THE SAVOY BOOK

**Edited by
David Britton & Michael Butterworth**

SAVOY

Published by Savoy Books Ltd., Manchester

ISBN 0 352 33001 5

Printed in Great Britain by The Anchor Press Ltd
Tiptree, Essex

This book is dedicated to the memory of
the late Elvis Presley (1954–1958) –
the most important figure of the twentieth century

Contents

THE SAVOY BOOK

Edited by
David Britton & Michael Butterworth

M. JOHN HARRISON

The Incalling

The Incalling was held somewhere in that warren of de-
feated streets which lies between Camden Road and St
Pancras, where the old men cough and spit their way
under the railway arches every evening to exercise their
fat dogs among the wet discarded fish-and-chip papers.
Clerk had made a great point of punctuality and then
failed to give me precise directions. I don't think he ex-
pected me to turn up at all. He had reached some crux
only partly visible to the outsider, and his life was terribly
muddled – a book was long overdue, he had been evicted
suddenly from his furnished flat in Harrow, he had a sense
of impending middle age which he obviously felt he
couldn't face without company of some sort; and beneath
all this was something deeper which he hinted at constantly
but refused to unveil. A publisher has a limited vocabu-
lary of responses to such a situation; to show him that I
knew my responsibilities I took him frequently to the pubs
and restaurants of Great Portland Street – where he in-
evitably ate little, seemed nervous, and instead of discuss-
ing the work in progress murmured almost inaudibly of
Frazer and Blavatsky, or his quarrels with G——, and
where, among the turned heads and plump shoulders of
lunching secretaries, his thin white acne'd face hovered
like the ghost of a child starved to death. I was curious;
he sensed this, and made energetic efforts to draw me in.
He was lonely; I wanted to help, of course, if I could, but

not from so intimate a distance; and lately our meetings had become memorable as a series of comically protracted farewells on station platforms and embarrassed hasty protestations of friendship made through the windows of departing taxicabs.

Anyway: I went to Camden that night not because I had any interest in the proceedings, but because I felt sorry for him, because lunches aren't enough, and because he was one of those people who can't seem to enjoy their follies without a sense of complicity. I would have accompanied him with equal enthusiasm to the Soho backstreet palace of his choice. Thanks to an unexplained delay on the North London Line I arrived shortly after the thing was due to begin, with no idea of exactly where it was to take place.

I found myself in a short empty crescent at one end of which stood a shuttered greengrocery – the pavement in front of it stacked with broken wooden boxes and some spoiled foreign fruit filling the cool air with a thick, yeasty odour while feral pigeons pecked about on the flagstones in the failing light – and at the other the second-hand clothes shop owned by Clerk's mentor, a woman of uncertain nationality who chose to call herself Mrs Sprake. This was a dim and oppressive cubbyhole with a cracked wardrobe mirror propped up against one wall, where faded tea-gowns hung limp and vacant behind the wire-screened windows like the inmates of a political prison for women. In the pre-war period it had been a 'corner café'; faded glass panels above the door advertised vanished soft drinks, and its atmosphere still felt etiolated as if from passage over gas burners on foggy November nights. Here I had to ask directions from the boy behind the counter, a fat-legged ten or eleven-year-old in short grey trousers who I imagined then to be Mrs Sprake's son – although now I'm not sure if their relationship could ever have been described so simply.

He was sucking something as I entered, and stooped quickly to take it out of his mouth, as if he were afraid whoever had come in might confiscate it. Over his shoulder I could see down a narrow passage to where a small television screen flickered silently and greyly in the gloom. A dog was moving about in another room. Clothing pressed in from all sides, dusty, touching my wrists. When I told him why I was there he stared into the mirror and said uninterestedly, "It's the fourth house down." His voice was peculiarly mature for his clothing and his pre-pubescent, sliding eyes. There was aniseed on his breath, and whatever he had been eating had left a brownish deposit, a small drying trickle in the downy hairs at the corner of his mouth. "Mr Clerk invited me," I explained, "but I forgot the way." He shrugged very slightly, and his hand moved behind the counter, but he said nothing more, and I doubted if he had ever taken any notice of the name. As I turned to go he had transferred his gaze to the distant television and, with a motion too quick to follow, had reclaimed his titbit and was chewing again.

On the way out I brushed against a stiff peach-coloured bodice covered with green sequins, to be startled by a sudden smell of the empty dance hall – some American perfume, faded and innocent; and beneath it, like a memory of austerity and the disingenuous festivals of a post-war Saturday night, the quick thin bitterness of chalk dust and ancient perspiration.

Much of the crescent was untenanted. In company with the surrounding streets it had been built as a genteel transit camp, matured as a ghetto, and now it was a long declining dream. I stood at the door of Mrs Sprake's house, staring at the cracked flags, the forgotten net curtains bunched and sagging like dirty ectoplasm, the tilted first floor balconies with their strange repetitive wrought iron figures, and wondering if it might not be better to leave now before any one had time to answer the bell. All the other doors were boarded up. Old paint hung like shredded wallpaper from the inner curve of an arched window. Across the road one whole building was missing from the terrace – fireplaces and outlines of extinct rooms clung to the walls of the flanking houses. I could telephone Clerk in the morning and tell him I hadn't been able to find the place; but it was too late now to go in search of a cinema, and too early for anything else; besides, the boy had seen me, and if I left I should look a fool.

Clerk himself opened the door, but not before I had heard footsteps approach, pause, and recede, then a woman's voice saying clearly, "We don't normally encourage gatherings," and, "He must come in, of course," on a rising, partly interrogative note.

His white face tilted out at me from the darkness of the hall, like the head of some long-necked animal thrust unexpectedly round the door. He looked tired and a little ill. Warmer air seemed to flow out past him, and for a second I was whirled along the sensory interface of outdoors and in, the one reeking of pulpy exotic fruit, the other of aniseed and dusty hessian, rushing together like incompatible ocean currents. The light of a single low-wattage lamp yellowed a passageway made narrow by piled teachests and bales of folded clothing, out of which the staircase, uncarpeted but thick with chocolate brown paint, ascended into a deeper gloom. It appeared to be a mere annex of the shop, and smelt so similar that I wondered if the chewing boy had somehow got ahead of me.

"Oh, hello, Austin," said Clerk. He blinked. "For a moment I thought you were someone else."

I was relieved to see him, but not for long. It was plain he'd made some sort of gaffe by inviting me and was regretting it. "You're late," he told me nervously; he said that I should 'try and fit myself in'; we had a ridiculous whispered misunderstanding over who should go first along the cramped hall. Finally he hurried me through into a small front parlour with bare white walls, where in preparation for the ceremony all the furniture had been shoved away from the centre of the room, exposing about ten square feet of freshly scrubbed unvarnished floorboards. On one side of the hall door were two ordinary wooden dining chairs, a spindly table between them draped with the same greyish imitation lace that hung before the window. Pushed up against the facing wall there was a two seat sofa covered in fawn PVC material, marked about the arms as by some cat or other small animal. A second door, opposite the window, led off into a scullery or kitchen, from which came the sound of water being run into a sink. On the sofa, quite still and ill-determined in the poor light, sat Alice Sprake.

Clerk introduced her proprietorially as 'the daughter of the house', becoming animated when he addressed her; she said nothing. She was eighteen or twenty years old and only her eyes, brown and unemotional, recalled her relationship to the boy in the clothes shop. She was vague. Although she looked levelly enough at me, I hardly felt the touch of her hand.

"I expect you're tired of waiting, are you?" I said brightly. Both of them ignored me, so I sat down. A small thickset woman wearing the perpetual mourning of the Greek Cypriot widow came through the scullery door. She was a little under middle age, but moved slowly as though her legs pained her; her face was thickly powdered in a strange lifeless orange colour; the sound of her breathing was quite plain in the room. She had under her arm one of those cheap religious pictures you see gathering dust in Catholic repositories, and this she proceeded to hang — with what seemed a great deal of effort — on a nail above the sofa. It was a Gethsemane, in the most lurid stereoscopic greys and greens. For a while I couldn't understand what was wrong with it; then I saw that it was upside down, the feeble soon-to-be-martyred face swimming out of it loose-mouthed and emotionally spent, staring into the room like a drowned man in a restaurant fish-tank.

"There," she said thickly. "That is that." She slumped on the sofa beside the girl, to stare exhaustedly at a spot on the wall above my head.

The silence drew out interminably. Clerk and I sat on the hard chairs; Alice Sprake and her mother sat on the sofa; nobody spoke, nothing was done. After a few minutes of this I realised that Clerk was staring so avidly at the girl that his eyes were watering. I couldn't see what absorbed him so. She belonged in some repository window herself, her flat adolescent face prim in the confinement of a gilt frame, the whole musculature immobile and stylised, the profile very slightly concave, the mouth so small and secretive. She had a dreamy manner certainly (which appeared at times to extend into an actual vagueness of physical presence – one might come into a room, I sensed, and spend ten minutes there before realising she was in it); but it was the unattractive fake dreaminess of the convent girl and the mass production madonna, the self-contemplatory lassitude of pubertal iron deficiency. I changed my opinion of Clerk's motives; then changed it back again, out of charity – he was oblivious, I felt like a voyeur; none of us after all understand our own motives. Mrs Sprake, meanwhile, twitched her feet – she sat sprawled back, hands limp at her sides – and seemed to be perfectly occupied with the wall. I tried to see through the grey net curtains. It was dark now in the street, but no lamps had come on. Someone walked slowly and heavily under the window, dragging footsteps close enough to be in the room. Clerk adjusted his spectacles, coughed. The drowned man mouthed at us from the iridescent gloom of his fish-tank. I couldn't bear it. "Er, why must the picture be upside down?" I said. "I suppose there's some particular significance to that?"

Clerk stared at me like a betrayed dog. The streetlights came on, filling the place with a dull orange glare.

Both women got up at once and left, Mrs Sprake going into the scullery, where she unlatched the back door, Alice into the hall. I heard retreating footsteps on the stairs, then the sound of someone coming in from the garden. The chewing boy put his head round the scullery door and gazed at the icon. Mrs Sprake reappeared standing on tiptoe behind him, looked straight at me and said, "You must kip silent, you understand? Kip very quiet." She cuffed the boy's ear. "You eat too much of that. There will be none left, and then what will you do?" And to me again, with what I thought must be pride, "My children are very good children, Mr Austin, very, very good. They do all their poor mother can't." The boy smiled at me with a mixture of shyness and impudence. He shifted his titbit from one side of his open mouth to the other, letting it pause for an instant on his stained tongue so I could almost see it. "Fetch the chalk then," he said, watching me closely. He had no vestige of her Mediterranean accent. The ghost of aniseed whispered from his mouth and reached into the corners of the room. "It can be done, Mr Clerk," called Mrs Sprake from the kitchen. "It has not been done for fifteen hundreds of years, but my children are clever children." Clerk looked dazed now that the girl had gone. He blinked at the boy. "Shut up and give me the chalk," said the boy.

He knelt down on the scrubbed floor and stared up at the icon, licking the half-inch or so of green chalk she had brought him. Suddenly he put it wholly in his mouth. When it came back it was pasty and covered with spittle, and the aniseed reek in the room had redoubled. He quickly used it to draw a large and irregular circle on the floor, shuffling along backwards on his haunches and dragging the hand with chalk in it along behind him. When he had completed this he sat in the middle of the circle for a second, his eyes vacant. Then he popped the chalk back into his mouth and seemed to swallow it entirely.

He got up stiffly and perched on the arm of the sofa, stretching his legs and grinning. One of his shoelaces had come undone. He caught my eye, made a little motion of the head to implicate me in some irony directed at Clerk, who had taken off his horn-rims, folded them carefully away, and was yearning toward the hall door with watery eyes. When I refused to join in, he shrugged and laughed quietly.

The door opened and back came Alice Sprake, to be trapped on Clerk's adhesive gaze like a small grey fly.

She went straight to the centre of the green chalk circle

and stood there, one leg relaxed, the other stiffened to take her weight. She had dressed in some sort of complicated muslin shift, the drooping skirts of which revealed the lower parts of her thighs. Her legs were short and plump, inexpertly shaved. Her feet were bare, the soles grubby. She brought with her faint odours of dust and perspiration; the decayed echo of *fin-de-siècle* water sprites and eurhythmical entertainments. She faced the boy as if waiting for a cue. The boy chewed and raised his hand. In the scullery Mrs Sprake switched on a small portable gramophone, which began to play an aimless, thready piece for violin and flute. With a shuffle and slap of bare feet on bare boards, Alice Sprake started to dance about in the chalk circle, her fixed and tranquil face now turned to Clerk, now to the reversed icon, now to the chewing boy. It was barely tolerable, but rather harmless at first. She waved her arms, trailing ectoplasmic fans of muslin in the peculiar light. She was a very poor dancer. Clerk had put his horn-rims back on; they followed her every movement, sodium light flashing from their lenses as he turned his head. Mrs Sprake leant on the door-frame with her arms folded, nodding to herself. The chewing boy let himself slide to the floor; back against the sofa, he drew one knee up to his chest, clasped it, and rocked himself to and fro. I coughed unhappily behind my hand, wondering how much Clerk had paid, and wishing I'd never seen him in my life.

But there was something wrong with the record player, and the music diminished steadily into a low, distant groan; the boy grew rigid (orange twilight limned his clenched jaw), while his mother let her arms fall to her sides, allowed all interest to leave her eyes; Clerk's expression became strained with greed. And abruptly Alice Sprake had ceased to be a village hall *danseuse* from some vanished Edwardian summer-twilight rehearsal, awkwardly pirouetting, heartbreakingly inept and weary, and was fluttering in what might have been real panic round and round the chalk circle, impaled and fluttering there on Clerk's stare, awash in the lurid glare beneath that drowned green man. The boy coughed painfully. Through clenched teeth he said, "Now, Mr Clerk!" His mother jerked awake and reached out her arm. Bleak white light flooded the room from an unshaded two hundred watt fitment in the ceiling. The drowned man leapt stereoscopically from his frame into the space above the sofa, caught open-mouthed in that act of unspeakable despair. The music ended, or became inaudible. Clerk scrambled to his feet and stepped into the circle. Alice Sprake made a strange writhing motion and pulled off her shift.

She began to trudge along the chalk line, round and round, compliant and bovine, Clerk not far behind, his eyes locked in that peculiar spasm of unsexual greed, fixed on her thin white back and low, pear-shaped buttocks. There was gooseflesh on her thighs, the light had bleached her pubic hair to a pathetic greyish tuft. Her degradation, it seemed to me, was complete: as was that of everybody else in the room. Her feet scraped interminably, and Clerk's scraped after. Round and round they went.

"Fucking hell, Clerk," I said. "You must be mad." I got up, meaning to wait for him outside – or perhaps not even to wait, or ever see him again. Mrs Sprake had vanished, but her son had now joined the endless shuffling procession in the centre of the room. As Clerk followed the girl, he followed Clerk. His jaws were rigid and he had forgotten his titbit. An unending trickle of brown fluid was running out of the corner of his mouth. Something perfectly intolerable and graceless was occurring. I slammed the front door and stood on the cooling pavement. My hands were shaking, but to this day I honestly believe it was out of fury. Clerk came out after about an hour, wiping his mouth as if he'd been ill. I don't know why I waited. Neither of us apologised for our behaviour. We went in silence down the High Street, past the alcoholics muttering behind locked news-stands, past the ticket office and down the moaning escalator, to be sucked into the echoing passages, the hot zones and sudden cold winds of the Camden Underground, to breath the thin dingy air of two separate carriages on the same train (and for all I know to read, with the same sensation of time suspended and an endless life under the earth, the same life-insurance posters and 'No Smoking' signs). We made no plans to meet again. I thought he seemed depressed and fearful, but that may have been a moral judgement.

Why he was indulging himself in so shabby a farce I couldn't conceive: but it was plain that none of his problems would be solved by encouraging it, so I sent a letter to the agency which represented him, reminding them that his book was due (indeed, long overdue), that our contract had been, if anything, overly generous as to completion dates, that we hoped he would soon see his way clear, and so on. I had given him up, or so I told myself, but I had my assistant sign it. A couple of days later they wrote to tell me that he had changed his address and they were having trouble getting hold of him.

As for the Sprakes, I couldn't think of them as having much existence at all outside the strained and grubby events of that evening. I imagined them as spending most of their time in a sort of dull stupor – immobile on a third-floor landing, looking mechanically down into a back garden full of rusty wheels, hard-packed earth and willow herb; silent and still behind the till of the second-hand clothes shop, eyes unfocused. I knew of course that they must get around the world somehow – shop for food, hurry along under the black rains of Camden to a supermarket (full of obscure longings, perhaps, for the similar skies of some Adriatic manufacturing hinterland), do the things ordinary people do – but saw them only as dreary, withdrawn and alien, lying perpetually but indifferently in wait for the credulous, rehearsing the curious frauds and crude new magic of the European industrial peasant, with its sodium-lit Catholicism and plastic iconolatry.

A langorous, unthinking contract exists between charlatan and victim, an understanding of which both are deeply aware. It didn't occur to me that there might be anything more to Clerk's obsession than the occasional reaffirmation of this covenant – until, about a month after the Incalling and out of an impulse I didn't understand, I found myself spying on him down by Charing Cross Pier.

It was a squally afternoon on the Victoria Embankment, one of those afternoons that wraps you one minute in a clinging mist of rain and the next surprises you with the pale lucid airs, the clarity and the depth of vision of quite another kind of day. The long arcs of Waterloo Bridge sprang out white and tense against the heavy blues and greys of the distant City. The river was agitated, high but falling under a cloudy sky. Gulls swirled in low flat circles over something in the water. The wind blew from Parliament, smelling of rain and fried food, and I was huddled in the shadow of the Gilbert memorial, waiting for a bus. A pleasure boat docked, a crowd developed on the covered gangways of the pier behind me – camera bags swinging, flapping nylon waterproofs, American and Japanese voices – and there he was, his white face unhealthy and out of place among all the tanned ones, his thin shoulders hunched and splotched with rain. He came up the oily black duckboards tearing his ticket in half and staring anxiously about him. I suppose I should have gone up to him and said hello; instead I turned my head away and pretended to be studying the plump complacent features of Frampton's bronze Gilbert, hoping to be taken for a sightseer and feeling enormously childish. My 168 arrived, pulled away without me.

I don't know why I did it. Something stealthy in his manner found an echo in my own. He was obviously waiting for someone; out of the corner of my eye I saw him go up to the confectionery kiosk by the railway bridge and hover uncertainly, glancing frequently back at the still-emptying boat as it wallowed at the pier.

A moment later Alice Sprake materialised at the head of the gangway and turned right toward Cleopatra's Needle. She passed not six inches away from me, head down in a dream, her hair blowing out from under a damp headscarf. She had on a dove-grey suit with a long skirt and puffed sleeves which in some former incarnation had belonged to a much older woman. Hurrying along the wide empty pavement under the lamp standards with their iron fish and strings of fairy lights, she looked like the wraith of a Victorian afternoon; and as she went, the band in Embankment Gardens struck up the march from Lincke's 'Father Rhine'. Clerk, too, passed close by me, his face a white smear between the sodden, turned-up points of his collar and his eyes so occupied with Alice Sprake I might have been a mile away. His trousers were soaked, his cheap shoes waterlogged, and he seemed to be shuddering with cold. He looked iller than I had ever seen him. I think she was quite unaware of what was going on. He kept about fifteen yards behind her, and when she showed signs of stopping or slowing became suddenly interested in a balk of rotting timber bobbing far out in the river. She vanished for a second or two then reappeared on the water stair of the Needle, aimless and innocent as any tourist. Rain blew round Clerk's dark lonely figure. When she left the stair and crossed the road, he drifted after her. The dripping trees of the gardens shook briefly in the wind, then closed over them.

I witnessed all this without surprise, feeling as detached as a man trying to follow, without benefit of commentary and through the condensation on a television dealer's window, the announcement of some foreign war: then, suddenly depressed, went over to the Charing Cross underground station and bought a ticket to Camden Town.

There, the sky was high, and for a moment at least, clear. If a wind blew down from Hampstead, it was a benign one; and as the old men dragged their dogs from intersection to intersection, the pavements were drying out. The blue-painted frontage of Mrs Sprake's shop looked shabby but less malicious in the watery light, although some reek or residuum of psychic exploitation seemed to hang in the air about it. No one moved in the street or behind the counter; the clothes were only old clothes; and the yeasty smell of spoiled fruit drifting down the crescent from the greengrocery made me quite hungry as I loitered on a nearby corner. I had been there for perhaps three quarters of an hour when Alice Sprake came into view, walking more quickly now and carrying a plastic Marks & Spencer's bag. She closed the door of the shop firmly behind her; a face appeared briefly at an upper window; emptiness seemed to grip the place more tightly than before.

A little later, Clerk hurried up and took station in the street. He shifted his feet uncomfortably and settled his raincoat closer about him, bending his long neck anxiously this way and that like a disturbed waterfowl; his gaze switched from tilted balcony to empty shop, then back again. What had brought him to shiver at a Camden kerbside, to stare at a dull and apparently vacant house, is still beyond me. Certainly, his association with the Sprakes was of longer standing than I then realised; and I think he had begun to follow the girl about the real world (the world, that is, outside the strained liberty and grubby constraints of the ritual) long before this incident took place – it was already habitual, instinctive. I found myself furious with him – with his miserable damp trouser legs, cracked suede shoes all cardboard and dye, his face like melting floor-wax – and not a little disgusted with my own morbid espionage. The smell of spoilt fruit plugged my throat. It was coming on to rain in heavy, isolated spots. I strode off down the crescent as though my anger alone might be sufficient to end the episode – reluctant for some reason to leave even as I wondered impatiently why on earth I had wasted my time, and not caring much if he saw me.

Nothing ended, however. I simply got lost among the unfamiliar backstreets beside Regent's Canal. I could find neither the tube station nor the North London Line; not even the High Street. I blundered angrily on to the canal towpath, and, with the dull green water full of greedy little fish on one side and the high decaying walls of a goods yard on the other, convinced myself I was walking toward Islington, not Camden at-all. I had to go further out of my way to get off it again, I wouldn't dare the nightmare brick waste east of York Way. The cloudbase lowered and the wind grew nasty, whipping across the lock basins, picking at the tethers of the crumbling boats and the plumage of a few miserable-looking ducks. Concrete steps rescued me finally, but now it was teeming with rain. I glimpsed from a distance like a beacon the curious Greek shops of Pratt Street and lost them again almost immediately. Then, wandering past the urns and stone draperies of a Victorian cemetery that had been turned into some sort of park – empty yellow swings, a child's roundabout gravely turning, sleepy alcoholics muttering the spirit's language from the benches – I caught a whiff of rotten fruit.

I was back at the end of the crescent. The light seemed to be fading already. I had lost an hour; and Clerk still stood patiently at his corner, like a tethered animal with its fur plastered down by the rain. Water streamed from his uptilted face. I thought I detected movement at an upper window – but Clerk's eyes were as vacant as the shop, and he seemed preoccupied by something else. It occurred to me that he wasn't strictly 'watching' anything: rather, it was as if he had got as close to some object as he possibly could, and was content just to be bobbing there at the interface until such time as he was able to penetrate it. Whatever it was, I left him there. A couple of streets away, I knew, the evening rush hour was beginning on a main road full of illuminated shop signs, tyres hissing through the wet. I turned toward it thankfully, feeling sympathetic (or so I described it to myself) and intrusive, willing to leave him to it without further comment, voiced or otherwise. I was, perhaps, simply relieved at having found someone familiar, if not comforting, among all those doomed wet streets. I was some yards along the pavement when he said suddenly and clearly, "Leave me alone, Austin. I know what you're up to."

When I looked back, astonished, he hadn't moved. The rain humiliated him and he stared on, that indefinable expression of need and illness pulling his face slowly out of shape, flesh into putty, into water and chaos.

A few days later the London summer set in like an infection. The air throbbed, and in less than a day grew thick and humid; by the next morning the traffic was piling it up and pushing it down Fitzroy Street into the Square, where it died before we had a chance to breath it. When Tottenham Court Road became sticky and intolerable after ten a.m., and my office untenable after eleven, I gave up and went to Scotland for a three week break. I didn't expect Clerk's dreary entanglements to follow me as far as the Buchaille Etive Mor, but the day I was due to leave I got a sour letter from him, and they did.

It was a peculiar letter, complicated, full of hidden accusations and reproofs. He was muddled, spoke of an illness – although he wasn't specific – and quoted extensively, for some reason I couldn't follow, from *Gerontion*. He made no reference to the Sprakes but went into detail about the 'insulting' letter he presumed had originated in my office, going on to attack his agent quite bitterly for forwarding it; and he left me in no doubt as to where our 'late' friendship stood. At least he had done some work – his completed manuscript came under separate covers. The agency rang me up that afternoon to ask me if I'd heard from him. "He won't answer the phone, and he's ignoring everything but cheques," they said, and seemed a bit hurt that he'd sent the book direct. Realising that I was about to be embroiled again, this time in some silly professional squabble, I left the whole thing with my assistant. "If they ring again, get them to try a registered letter," I told him. "I'm not Clerk's keeper." But it had begun to look as if I was, and he only grinned cynically. "There can't be much wrong with him if he's cashing his bloody cheques." So I spent a good part of my holiday trying to forget Eliot's eerie, and when I got back, found Clerk's manuscript still cluttering up the office. "You should have a look at that," said my assistant maliciously. "They won't typeset from that. I didn't really know what to do with it. It hasn't even got a title." I sighed and took it home that night and couldn't read more than a couple of pages – the typescript was scrawled all over with illegible corrections in a peculiar brownish ink, and I couldn't tell whether it was a novel disguised as a memoir or a diary disguised as a novel. "I'll have to go and see him about it, I suppose." "More fool you."

Clerk now lived somewhere in the bedsitter belt of Tufnell Park. Fool or not, I caught a bus over there, the manuscript under my arm in a box meant for foolscap typing paper. It was shortly before dusk at the end of a protracted, airless August: my sinuses ached, and the evening wind curling between the rows of tall shabby houses was no relief – it stirred briefly, nuzzling at the gutters where it found only the dust and heat of a month past, then settled down like an exhausted dog. Five or six bellpushes were tacked up by the outer door. I worked them in turn but no one answered. A few withered geraniums rustled uneasily in a second-floor window box. I pushed the door and it opened. In some places we're all ghosts. I swam aimlessly about in the heat of the hall, knocking and getting no response. Up on the first floor landing a woman stood in a patch of yellow light and folded her arms to watch me pass; in the room behind her was a television, and a child calling out in thin excitement.

Clerk lived right at the top of the stairs where the heat was thickest, in three unconnected rooms. I tapped experimentally on each open door in turn. "Clerk?" Empty jam jars glimmered from the kitchen shelves, the wallpaper bulged sadly in the corner above the sink, and on the table was a note saying, 'Milk, bread, catfood, bacon,' the last two items heavily underlined and the writing not Clerk's. A lavatory flushed distantly as I went into what seemed to be his study, where everything had an untouched, dusty look. "Clerk?" Bills and letters were strewn over the cracked pink linoleum, a pathetic and personal detritus of final demands which I tried furiously to ignore; it was too intimate a perspective – all along he had forced me to see too much of himself, he had protected himself in no way. "Clerk!" I called. From his desk – if he ever sat at it – he had a view of the walled garden far below, choked like an ancient pool with elder and *Colutea arborescens* and filling up steadily with the coming night. It was very quiet. "Clerk?"

He had come silently up the stairs while I poked about among his things and was now standing at the window of the bedsitting room, peering round the curtain into the street. I fidgeted in the doorway, holding the manuscript in front of me like a fool. "Clerk?" He knew perfectly well that I was there but he wanted me to see that the street was more important. Between us the room stretched dim and bleak: a bed with its top cover pulled back, some things arranged on top of a chest of drawers, books and magazines stacked haphazardly along the skirting boards. He had done nothing to make the place comfortable. A suitcase stood in the middle of the floor as if he'd simply left it there the day he moved in.

"I rang the bell," I said, "but nobody came."

He stared harder into the street.

"So you made yourself at home anyway," he said. He shivered suddenly and jerked the curtains closed. "You've got a bloody nerve, Austin, following me around . . ." On the verge of developing this he shrugged and only repeated, "A bloody nerve," then sat down tiredly on the bed, looking at his hands, the vile cabbage-rose wallpaper, anything but me. With the curtains drawn the room became much larger and vaguer, filling up with vinegar-coloured gloom. I could hardly see him. "What do you want, then?" he asked, apparently surprised to find me still there. "I'm on my own all bloody day, then people come just when I don't care to be bothered with them."

I wanted to leave him to it, abandon him to the cabbage roses, 'Milk, bread, catfood,' and the *Psychic News*, and go home. Instead I held the manuscript up like a charm or entry permit and went into the gloom where he waited for me. He had become a spectre of himself. His miserable, aggressive face bobbed about above the bed, a tethered white balloon, what flesh remained to it clinging like lumps of yellow plasticine at cheekbone and jaw, the temples sunken, the whites of the eyes mucous and protuberant. He was wearing the bottom half of a pair of striped pyjamas, his stomach bulging out over the drawcord like some atrocious pregnancy while the rest of his body seemed reduced, temporary, all skin and bone. If the pursuit of Alice Sprake from Charing Cross to Camden had sickened him, where had he followed her since, and how far, to make him look like this? I was filled equally with repugnance and compassion, and in fighting both only made myself seem mealy mouthed and foolish.

"Look," I admitted, "you're not at all well, and I realise this is inconvenient. But we really ought to discuss this book. It could be really fine, I'm sure, if we just clarify a few things, a really fine book." This was rubbish, of course, and I could hear my assistant laughing sardonically somewhere in the more honest places of my skull. Not that I imagined Clerk would swallow it, but a publisher has his duties . . . and I had some idea of cheering him up, I suppose, as an easy solution to my own embarrassment. "Why don't you get back into bed and take it easy while I make some coffee or something? Then we can thrash it out . . ."

He laughed quietly to himself, whether at my expense or his own I wasn't sure.

"Suit yourself, Austin. Make as much coffee as you like. I'm going to sleep. You're a patronising bastard but I'm sure you know that already."

I dropped the manuscript on the end of the bed, preparing to walk out and wash my hands of him. But it was something of a victory to have got him to talk to me at all, and somehow I found myself in the kitchen, pottering about among the dirty cups and staring out into the garden as I waited for the water to boil. I had to put money in the gas. There was an extraordinary staleness in the air, as if no one had lived there for years, and I wondered if he'd cooked himself anything to eat that day, or even the day before. Milk, bread and catfood, but the milk was off, the cat gone, and the bread mouldy: and down in the garden twilight piling up among the elder boughs. I heard him moving about in the bedsitting room, muttering to himself. "You don't mind black coffee?" I called. When I got back with the tray I found him sitting up in bed. He had taken the manuscript out of its box and scattered it all over the room.

"Go on, Austin," he taunted, "be reasonable about *that*. Perhaps we could have some tea next, eh?" He had tried to tear the thing in half before throwing it about, but his only success had been to crumple a few sheets at either end. I put the tray down and went round on my knees picking pages up at random while he stared at me with dislike and misery. I had the feeling, there in the half-dark full of his desperation and my feebleness, that his head and neck had become detached somehow from his shoulders and were weaving independently about over the bed, sick and lost. "I don't want your coffee. I don't want your advice. I won't make any changes, Austin, so forget it. Take the bloody thing as it is or leave it there on the floor. Just get out, that's all."

"Clerk, you're ill . . ."

I thought he was going to hit me. The tray went over with a crash, spraying hot coffee over my legs. He struggled to his feet, and, wearing a great tangle of bed linen like a cloak, came half-running half-falling towards me, arms outstretched and fingers hooked – only to turn aside at the last instant and head for the window, where he writhed his shoulders free of the dirty topsheet and

Dutch blanket, tore the curtains completely off their runners and stared into the street as if his life depended on the next thing he saw, shaking and sweating and shouting, "Fuck off!", over and over again.

"Christ, Clerk . . ."

". . . off, fuck off, fuck off, fuck off, fuck . . ."

I pushed him aside. It was dark, and the sodium lamps had flared up like a forgotten war. Ten or fifteen yards away across the road, shadowy in the disastrous orange glare, his face turned up to study the window and his jaws moving firmly and rhythmically from side to side, Mrs Sprake's son sat kicking his heels on a low garden wall. Dark shrubbery moved behind him. He looked straight at me, I thought, and nodded. The room was silent. Coffee dribbled down my calf, sticky and cooling. Beside me, Clerk had closed his eyes and was resting his forehead against the window pane. I felt his hip tremble suddenly against me, but I couldn't get my eyes off the boy in the street.

"Is this what's making you ill?" I asked. "Being mixed up with this spiritualist stuff?" I had some mad idea that they might be drugging or blackmailing him.

Clerk groaned. "What on earth are you talking about, Austin?" he said wearily. He let himself slide to the floor. Kneeling amid the debris of his book, holding on to the window frame, he made an odd gurgling noise. He turned his head away. At first I thought he was laughing. Then I realised he was being sick. He panted and coughed, his thin shoulders heaving.

"I've got cancer, you bloody fool," he said. "I've had it for two years. The Sprakes are my only hope . . . so just go away now, will you?"

I left him there, wiping his mouth on a sheet of the manuscript and staring vacantly ahead as if he were dead already, and rushed out of the place. I was choking with nausea, self-disgust, and an anger I could barely contain. The woman on the landing was waiting for me, arms still folded. "He's poorly is he, Doctor?" she said, "I thought so," and shook her head slowly. "I hope it's not catching . . ." She stood in my way while, above, Clerk sobbed dryly. I knew he was staring out of the window again, eyes wide in that swollen papier-mâche puppet's face. "Excuse me," I said. But when I got to the doorstep the chewing boy was nowhere to be seen. I ran across the road and looked into the bushes, which were still moving. It was the wind. I stood there for a moment. Tufnell Park was like a grave. I could hear faint, running footsteps a street away. At least I had the advantage of knowing where the child would go.

It's hard to say what made me so angry. Perhaps it was that Clerk should have to relinquish the world clutching only memories of that grubby little ceremony; that his despair should bequeath him in the end only endless puzzling images of the waste land between Camden and King's Cross Station, with its tottering houses and its old men spitting in corners full of ancient dust each grain of which has begun as dog-dirt or vomit or decayed food; that he could be promised only the fakery of sodium light, the deadly curve of the crescent and the far-off buzz of the traffic beyond Mrs Sprake's second-hand clothes shop. I couldn't quite separate compassion and personal outrage, and I don't suppose I ever shall. I went after the boy because I couldn't bear to think of a dying man made confused and hateful by charlatans . . . and, again, to silence a part of me which understood this: where human sympathy is absent it can't easily be replaced by lunch in Great Portland Street.

He got home before me, of course, and by the time I reached the crescent it was deserted but for the eternal reek of smashed fruit (and behind that, something old, foggy, a smell which belonged to the same street, certainly, but in an unfamiliar time). I went to the house first and banged loudly on the door, but there was no reply. I shouted, but all that achieved was echoes, "Mrs Sprake! Mrs Sprake!" racing away over acres of railway siding, dull canal water and decaying squares, until I had a vision of my cries travelling perfect and undiminished all the way to Islington, as if the whole universe were suddenly dark, uninhabited, and sensitive to the slightest sound. After a minute or two of this I tried tapping on the front room window instead. Then I put my eye to a gap in the net curtain.

Mrs Sprake was in there, sprawled heavily on the sofa with the light turned off, arms limp at her sides. She had rolled her skirt up to her waist and her stockings down to her knees. On the wall in front of her hung the same cheap icon she had employed for the Incalling . . . had her eyes been open, they would have been focused on it. Perhaps they were focussed on it anyway. The doomed man yearned down at her from his showcase, but her face was slack and expressionless. Beneath the horrible orange powder and soft, pitted skin lay an ignorance and indifference so intense as to seem avid, an abrogation, a vacancy, and a frightening weariness. I stared in astonishment at her exposed belly and thick white thighs; then rapped the window so hard it cracked under my knuckles. At the sound of this she opened her eyes suddenly and peered in my direction; her lips moved exhaustedly, like those of a sick fish. I was terrified I might somehow discover exactly what I had interrupted. I shouted "Open up!" or something equally useless, but moved off hurriedly down the street before she had a chance to comply.

In the dim grey wash of light from a forty-watt bulb inside, I fought briefly with the door of the shop; it gave only to my full weight, and then so suddenly that I went down heavily on one knee over the threshold.

Nobody was there. From the passage behind the counter, where the air was lax and hot, issued a smell of time, dust and artificial flowers (then, worked through that like a live thread, the distant familiar stink of the boy); and the television still flickered silently in its back room, as if nobody had bothered to turn it off since my last visit. "Hello?" I went through and stood there in the fitful pewter glow, rubbing my bruised leg. If I put my ear close to the television I could hear it whisper, "So far we have managed to avoid this." "I know you're here!" I called. I knew nothing. Except for Mrs Sprake at her inexplicable devotions the universe was still uninhabited . . . dolorous, scoured, yet waiting to respond instantly to some crude signal I couldn't give . . . I felt abandoned to it, left for dead. I drifted toward the staircase in the corner, then up it, the heat pressing against my chest like a firm dry hand.

The whole top floor, knocked into one large room and all but one of its windows bricked up twenty or thirty years before, had been given over to him. The furniture was a clutter of the ricketty stuff you can find any day in the junk shops towards Chalk Farm; a bed, a dresser, some bentwood chairs. On the dresser was a pile of what looked like grey feathers, and pushed away in one corner were some stuffed animals mounted on bits of wood. It all looked dreary and neglected . . . uninhabited, and yet at the same time as if he spent most of his life there. He was squatting on the bare floor watching me intently, his pudgy hands on his knees. "There's nothing for you here, Mr Austin," he said. "Why don't you go home?"

"You don't know what I came for. Besides, I'd rather speak to whoever's responsible for you . . . your mother, if you can wake her up."

He moved his jaws once, mechanically.

"You're horrified, Mr Austin, and who can blame you? It was immaterial to you what Clerk did with his life. Now you find you can't ignore him any longer, and you care what he does with his death. Good!" In front of him on a low occasional table he had arranged a fragment of mirror, two ordinary white candles, and an old bottle dug up from some Victorian towpath: all positioned so that when he looked into the glass the twin unsteady flames underlit his face without themselves being reflected. "Good! It's never too late to feel compassion . . ." And he smiled suddenly, rubbing his hands on his knees . . .

"You're safe! *You* need nothing we have here!" The bottle contained a few inches of cloudy preservative. Floating in that was something which looked like a thick, contorted black root. It was corked, but even so every fibre of the grey floorboards and white plaster, every bit of furniture, had soaked up the reek of aniseed . . . now they gave it back into the air like a fog, to fill the mouth and coat every delicate membrane of the nose. "Later you may discover your compassion is not as pure as you imagine, or your rage for justice; but for the moment . . . We're all revolted by illness, Mr Austin, revolted and frightened . . . There's no reason on Earth to feel ashamed of that!"

For a moment he gave his attention to the little altar, and when he spoke again his voice was thoughtful and cold. "I know exactly why you're here, you see. You came for reassurance. In any case it was useless to bother. Go home now."

I went over to the window, but it wouldn't open. Outside was that absorbent, sodium-lit vacancy, stretching all the way to Islington. If I concentrated, I could hear something that might have been traffic on Camden High Street. I tried breathing deeply to acclimatise myself to the stink, but that only made me feel worse. "I'm not leaving here until I know what you promised him," I said, "and what your mother charged him for it. It's a grubby fraud and I'll have it stopped . . ."

"Leave the window alone!" He swivelled round irritably, his pudgy legs suddenly shooting out in front of him. He stood up and came rapidly across the room. "My mother is shit, Mr Austin, under my feet. Why do you keep going on about her? I give her this!" And he writhed the fingers of his right hand. He stared up at me. "Why don't you go home?" he said savagely. "I don't want you here. Clerk? Clerk is shit too . . ." He shrugged. "What do I care? We gave him nothing he didn't want. He's a tinkerer."

Nothing moved in the street.

"Christ," I said softly, "you little brat, you."

I tried to catch hold of his shoulder, but somehow my hand made no contact. He twisted from under it and ran off a few steps. When he turned back his face was as I'd first seen it, blank and uninterested, hardly even self-involved. "Fucking cunt pig," he said distinctly, without any human emphasis. He began chewing rapidly. "Fucking cunt pig." He went and sat down in front of his altar, hunching his shoulders and gazing into the mirror. The whole room forgot me and filled up with silence. He laughed, then coughed urgently. "The window, Mr Austin!" he hissed. He seemed to be having some sort of choking fit. "Go on!"

I stared down into that hopeless little landscape of death, at the blistered paint, the gaps between the houses and the ancient rubbish in the gutters. Nothing. Then Alice Sprake walked sedately into view on the other side of the street, with Clerk drifting along in her wake like a dead waterfowl. She was wearing the same dove-grey skirt I had seen on the Embankment, and her prim adolescent features were dreamy, secretive. He had put his raincoat on but was otherwise as I had seen him an hour before . . . and down from its hem poked his long scrawny legs in their striped pyjama trousers. His feet were bare. I watched her draw him along behind her at a steadily increasing pace toward St Pancras. They never once looked up. He was very close to her as they were sucked out of sight, but she didn't seem to know he was there, or sense in any way his white awful face bobbing loosely about over her shoulder, his gaping pain and greed. In a moment the universe was uninhabited again and they pulled deep into it toward some crux of railway lines and dark water.

Behind me the chewing boy stretched his arms and scuffed his feet. He yawned. "You see?" he said. "Go home now, Mr Austin," he added, almost kindly. "There's nothing you can do for him. You never could."

I went across to him and kicked the table over. The mirror broke: the bottle fell on the floor and came uncorked: the candles tumbled end over end through the brown and stinking air. I bent down and hit him while he sat there, as hard as I could on the left cheek.

"Speak like a child," I said.

He rolled about in the mess spilt from the bottle, making a high, thin chuckling sound, then lay there grinning up at me. His head rolled to one side, he let his mouth fall open and brown fluid gushed down his chin. He chewed and chewed.

"Yes, sir?" he enquired. "Do you want to buy something or sell something? My mother isn't available presently for buying, but I am allowed to sell. We buy and sell all kinds of garments, sir . . ."

I ran out after Clerk and the girl but I never caught up with them.

Clerk died perhaps two months later, somewhere in the black end of a rainy November; slipping over the edge of a pulmonary complication at two in the morning, that hour which erodes all determination and wears the confused substance to a stub. The cancer had eaten his insides entirely away, but he was trying to correct the manuscript of the novel which finally appeared last week as *The World Reversed* (a title suggested by my assistant). We discovered the following pencilled against the opening sentences of Chapter Eight: 'When the dead look back, if they look back on us at all, they do so without rancour or pity, sadness or any sense of the waste of it. They crumble too soon and become too much a minute part of events to have any more involvement with us, and waste quickly away like footmarks on an oily pavement in October. This I know, though not from personal experience. Yet their evaporation is continual, they boil up continually around us, we inhale them as we go, and each resultant outward breath impregnates the soft brick of the city like smoke, dampens every blown newspaper, and as a curious acidic moisture loosens the pigeon dung on the ledges above . . .' There is more, but the handwriting is difficult to interpret.

On the night he died, or it may have been a couple of nights later, I had this dream . . .

I was walking along the grass verge of some provincial road, one of those roads which always seem empty and bleak, the hedges crusted at their roots with a thin grey mud thrown up by the wheels of passing vehicles, the fields on either side empty of livestock yet cropped short, the isolated houses unlit and shut up; a landscape apparently untenanted but showing signs of a continual invisible use. It was dark, but not night. Light had been bleached out of the still air and drained from all objects so that although there was no reversal of contrast the scene had about it the feel of a photographic negative. Walking beside me in her dove-grey suit, her head bowed and prim, her expression at once placid and secretive, was Mrs Sprake's daughter, Alice. Why I should have been so close to her, whether there was any feeling between us, I can't say. It seems unlike me. Her bovine calm had repelled me – and still does – when awake; but we cannot be responsible for what we feel in dreams. What is clear is that I felt a sense of unease on her behalf, and turned continually to stare backward at the distant figure which followed us.

"We should have a pleasant time," she said. Awake, I cannot imagine this; but I remember it clearly.

"You had better go ahead of me," I told her, and we walked like that for some minutes, in single file, while our pursuer remained a mote of energy in the middle distance, trotting doggedly along but seeming to make no headway. After a little while we were drawn into the outskirts of a small dull manufacturing town, along a protracted, gently curving dual carriageway, lined with the semi-detached houses and bleak recessed shop fronts of some postwar ribbon development. Through the gaps in the houses I glimpsed the vacant cinders of a transport café car park, puddled and luminous; then a scrapyard full of bluish moonlight, and a canal, and a crematorium in a muddy park. There was no wind or noise. I imagined the road falling into darkness behind us as we went, each traffic intersection, each garage with its peculiar rusted petrol pumps and abandoned forecourt dissolving into the vacuum through which our pursuer flailed his way, panting and groaning as he fought his own dissolution. When I looked again, he was no closer. I began to drag Alice Sprake along none the less, urging her with, "We must hurry", and, "Please do hurry."

There was no relief to be had from the vast silent space beyond the thin crust of buildings. It was uninhabited and smelt faintly of burnt rubber and ancient summer dust, it was a mere magnetic emptiness which had drawn us there simply for the sake of being there. Ages seemed to pass. If there were echoes of our quickening pace, they came back transmuted from that vacancy which is the source of everything, and we did not recognise them. Eventually it became plain that the curving road was merely an enormous circle, and all that part of it we had already walked only a few degrees of arc. Later still, the scrapyard passed again, the distant sports fields and crematorium, the cinders and the puddled forecourts and the hanging signs. Within the circle and without it were only acres of unemotional darkness, dragging at the footsteps of old men and invalids, sifting down to end as dust in gutters at windy corners, absorbent of all effort, all anxiety, all movement except that of the desperate creature behind us. I glanced back to make sure that he remained in the middle distance, held there by his very effort to progress . . .

I glanced back, and he was at my heels, his face Clerk's, looming white and pasty like melting floor wax over my shoulder an inch from my own, bobbing and weaving on the end of that pale rubbery stalk. His eyes were huge and avid, full of terror, his huge mouth vomited brown fluid, an abcess of misery and desire so close I knew it must burst and soak me. At the instant of touching, between the cup and the lip, that bleak image of the provinces flew apart and faded, as if he had brought with him landscapes of his own, a thin envelope of relics to insulate against the vacuum. Late taxicabs and midday restaurants formed briefly around us only to evaporate and give way to the Sprake's front room, the watery, quivering purlieus of Embankment Gardens and finally the cracked pink linoleum, the walled garden, the cabbage roses, the milk, bread and catfood of his rented grave in Tufnell Park, the thinning atmosphere of self-disgust which had sustained him in desolation. "I'm on my own all bloody day," he whispered, "My bloody day . . ." I winced away, afraid of some infinite prolongation of our last, hopeless meeting; yet in that moment felt whatever substance he now had left to him dissolve: and like smoke sucked from some distant corner of the room toward the hearth he was drawn through me and into Alice Sprake, who waited on the green chalk line, bovine and compliant, all grey degraded gooseflesh and grubby feet, one ill-shaved leg stiffened to take her weight. She made no move at the moment of penetration, and he was absorbed. I woke up sweating in a pale grey dawn with a faint, remote sound of shunting engines dying in my skull, and stayed at home that day.

I give this for what it is worth: as a completion, perhaps. But if you take it as such, you must remember that it is a personal one, and I draw nothing from it in the way of a conclusion. I never knew what the Incalling was supposed to achieve – or even whether what I witnessed in Camden represented failure or success. Clerk had said that the Sprakes were his last hope: on the evidence, their crude urban magic doesn't seem to have done him much good. He is, after all, dead. Perhaps it would have worked better elsewhere in Europe, where they still have some small link with older traditions. My own part in it, if I can be said to have had one, I would prefer to forget.

R. JENKINS NOV. 1976

HEATHCOTE WILLIAMS

Natty Hallelujah

"*Il n'y a pas une danse comme la décadence.*"

"Mmmmn."

"Champagne? Every bubble was put in by hand."

"Mmmmn."

Coon took the glass and drank it and then slipped his crank into Miss Tresses holy cavern, dreaming of tickling trout. His whole body was a hand catching the finest silver flyer by its gills in pitch darkness. Psychotropic splinters shot through his auric pores. She was a particle accelerator, churning and milling and creaming Olympian sperm that had bypassed her womb in favour of a stranger immortality in the occult glands of her brain.

Squeeze. Charver. Felch. Melt.

Bad fucks reincarnate Janus. Good fucks intertwine the lovers' brain-stems like the alchemical serpents twisting round the Caducean stave of power.

One tribe believes that some children are born blind because their parents wouldn't look each other in the eyes when they were making it. It? Luring down the god-head. Receiving instructions. The intertwining brain-stems are a potent aerial for divine messages.

It could be argued, Coon thought, that all human activity is a substitute for a good fuck: there is food there, light, shelter, yoga and adventure . . .

Miss Tresses licked his piece clean in case there should have been any tardy sperm there needing a higher home,

---

and Coon turned to a pile of books for some post-priapal reading.

An odd glow came from a book called the Gnostic Gospel according to Thomas. He pinched it out of the and read:

'His disciples said: "When wilt Thou be revealed to us and when shall we see Thee?" Jesus said: "When you take off your clothing without being ashamed, and take your clothes and put them under your feet as the little children and tread on them, then shall you behold the Son of the Living One and you shall not fear." '

Coon was six foot five, and was brought up in Belmont, Port of Spain, Trinidad. He was darker than all his family. When *Raas Class Blood Clot Man* fell on deaf ears, his mother called him shit-skin, usually when she was drunk at the end of carnival and she had spitefully christened him Coon. He left home for the sea at the age of thirteen, and never returned, ending up for the longest time of all in Morocco amongst Gnaoua musicians who always played their music for a purpose, and who were often accompanied by magicians who drank boiling water and ate live snakes.

He had been drawn towards Islam. Muhammed, it was rumoured amongst the Berbers, was to be reborn in the body of a man. It explained their flowing djellabas. They were all prepared for the pregnancy.

Miss Tresses played a record called *Babel*. The cover showed a large orange Mercedes truck converted to look like a mobile mosque. 'Recorded in Ruijgoord, Rough Place, by anonymous nomads *en route* to El Aiun. Play this record loud, squat your neighbours' ears. *Laissez paître votre paix*. The sky begins on the ground.' An English voice was chanting with a background of tam-tams, gongs and gimris, and dervish reeds: "It's a Bomber's Moon! Bad vibes gonna get their come-uppance soon! Buildings cannot scream! Time to plumb the anarchist pipe-dream! A pound of weedkiller, and a pint of Co-op sugar, pack 'em up together in an old Cortina!

Palaces! Banks! Copshops! (*explosions in the background*). Buildings Cannot Scream! There's doom-dots on the walls – An H-Bomb on the door, you're welcome to come round, but you won't come round no more. King Mob Rules. OK? The Priesthood is Armed. THE PRIESTHOOD IS ARMED!"

Coon and Miss Tresses basked for a few seconds in the push-me pull-you of intermingling eye-beams, and then Coon bowed, touched his heart, and walked out of the door.

Walking past the pedestrian precinct by Our Lady of Walsingham in Powis Square he was accosted by a group of rotting cider bums: "Mister, mister, come here . . . do us a favour, will you, we just need ten pee to get ourselves another bottle."

"Tell me something I don't know, and I'll give you everything I have."

"Oh, that's . . . that's a hard one . . . tell you something. I mean you seem an educated man," he said in a wheedling, ingratiating manner. "Come on now, mister, give us the ten pee."

"Tell me something amusing, that I haven't heard before, and I'll give you ten pee."

"Oh, a joke, yeah, a joke . . . listen, listen there was this Irishman . . . PADDY! What was that joke about the Irishman and the Everest expedition and them running out of scaffolding?"

But Coon had turned away.

'There's a certain plant in Spain,' Coon thought, 'which lives entirely on meteor dust. The Sun beats, it expands and contracts, every four hours and twenty seconds. How do you tell a Polish Lesbian? She likes men.' Anything along those lines would have satisfied him. He disappeared round the corner.

None of the drunks in their frazzled quest for funds had noticed that he was naked.

The Emperor's Old Clothes fitted perfectly. There's a bacteria which attacks concrete, and Coon began to exude them from his soles, turning the hard paving stones under his feet into a friendly mulch.

He hailed a cab. "Where do you want to go?"

"Where do *you* want to go? IGNORE ALIEN ORDERS."

The cabbie laughed, threw up his hands, nodded his head almost diagonally as the Indians do, a gesture which means 'Yes' and 'No' at the same time, and also conveys a sense of cosmic awe, and then laughed again.

Coon got in.

The cabbie steamed up to Notting Hill Gate with an 'In for a penny, in for a pound' expression on his face, and a flitting thought which also kept him going, that perhaps this was all part of a movie he hadn't heard about. Eventually he spoke again over his shoulders.

"You seem to know all the answers. What the fuck's going to happen?"

Coon didn't answer. The cabbie drove on and then plucked up the courage to deliver another mini-salvo.

"I mean what do you do for a living? I mean . . . Well, how are you gonna pay for this ride? You don't seem to have the wherewithal to be quite honest."

"What do *you* do for a living?" Coon said, "assuming you're alive."

The cabbie looked up in the driving mirror at the Moorish giant, but he wasn't there.

Coon had formed his hands into a psychokinetic mudra, and transplanted the cabbie into the back seat, and himself into the driver's compartment, turning on the light that proclaimed the cab was for hire.

The cab driver didn't seem particularly thrown, but after years of doing the same thing over and over again, accepted that something in the cab had gone into fifth, sixth, or even seventh gear, and started answering some of the questions that he'd originally put when he was in the front of the cab, from the back.

"What's going to happen to us? We're going to die!"

"We're going to *die*?" said Coon, "who told you we were going to die?"

"People."

"PEOPLE?? You trust PEOPLE!!"

"How am I going to pay the fare?" said Coon, a little later.

"I don't know," said the cabbie, "there's some money in the front."

Coon stopped the cab at a parking meter, wrenched off the top, poured the contents into the cabbie's hands and drove on. "These metal flowers grow everywhere, converting every street into a People's Raas Bank."

Shortly they were in Knightsbridge. A green-liveried commissionaire outside Harrods hailed the cab.

"Take these people to the Hilton Hotel, will you?" he said in a military manner.

"What makes you think I wanna waste precious calories ferrying overprivileged consumers to that laughable slum," said Coon.

"Look, you, don't be funny with me, otherwise I'll have you off the streets. You got your fuckin' sign out, haven't you?"

Coon opened the cab door, discreetly modelling for the taxi queue, climbed out and strode up to the commissionaire.

"Yes. I got my sign out."

"What is this, you gone mad or something?"

Coon lifted the commissionaire above his shoulders and tore off his braided, sub-martial frippery. He stripped him down to the buff, and then carried him through the marbled entrance, and planted him petrified in one of the window displays, weaving a flickering hand round his head, murmuring: "Be Here Now," and returned to the cab.

The cabbie was almost apoplectic with mirth. Coon rolled the cab slowly down the queue, finding a couple who'd just joined it at the end, and who alighted, storing their carrier bags and luggage in the compartment next to

Coon. He glanced at the contents of one of the bags and saw an object marked *Fabrica Modette, Exclusive Eurolux Styling*, and from it formed an impression of the travellers.

Coon flashed an ad on to the dicky seat facing the three passengers: 'Capitalists use whatever fertiliser they can to grow capital, and the best fertiliser is corpses. Raas Department of the Environment.' He noticed it catch their eyes, and then drove like Jehu.

"Tourists?" said the cabbie in the back.

"Just passing through," the couple replied. "We . . . er . . . we didn't quite realise we had to share this taxi."

The cabbie had been on the floor of the cab, mildly out of his lid when they got in.

"Where are we going?"

"Oh, there and back," said the cabbie, giggling, and shaking his head with his mouth open.

Coon kept one ear on the conversation at the back and one on the cab radio. He'd developed the facility of blinking his earlids, flapping them closed when there was nothing in the outside world worthy of his attention, and his inner voices seemed paramount. The technique went unnoticed beneath his long rastafarian locks.

The conversation at the back seemed to be a bit flat, so he changed channels and kept one ear on his inner voice and the other on the radio.

Inner voice: Jah is cally. Jah children are iry children. Blessed is the pipe of peace that is kept alight in the house of Jah in the valley of Zion.

Radio: Due to the decline in population of the gorilla there have been several attempts lately to breed the gorilla in captivity. Guy the gorilla at London Zoo was introduced to a female, but unfortunately showed no interest. Officials of the Royal Zoological Society then took the curious but imaginative step of showing blue movies to the two gorillas with the result that the female gorilla, Lettuce, attempted to seduce the projectionist.

"Did you hear that?" said Coon laughing, to the couple over his shoulders.

"No, I'm sorry . . . what was that?" said the man, who was wearing a cosy camel-hair coat, and carried a brief-case with about three locks on it, which never left his pink palms.

"Look," said the man nervously, "where are we going?" He clutched the brief-case tighter, suddenly feeling that something had gone out of it. It hadn't. But the locks had been slid aside with a Houdini breath from the front.

"We're going to the Zoo," said Coon, and then, mercurially sussing that the largest ingredient of the brief-case was dollar bills, added: "Were you aware, little pink brother, that the largest ingredient of bank notepaper was Indian Hemp? It'll soon be cheaper to smoke money. That could also be the reason why money is physically addictive as well as psychically. Pass a wad through the hatch and we'll do some market research."

At the next set of traffic lights, the man tried the cab doors, but they'd done a contrapuntal descant to the locks on his brief-case and jammed . . . a Hi-Jack. The man caught sight of a blind match-seller with thick dark glasses, and prayed for him to turn into two Moshe Dayans.

"Look. I don't know whether it'll make any difference, but I want to tell you who I am. I'm the assistant under-consul at the Paraguayan embassy, and I have to be back there in fifteen minutes. I'll make it worth your while. I don't know what this is about, and I don't care."

Coon started singing cryptically and quite irrelevantly: "There ain't no truth to Ruth, if she gotta broken tooth," but it turned out that Ruth was the woman's name. She looked at her husband in desperation.

Coon rolled a massive splif and blew clouds of ganja gremlins through the hatch. "Assistant under-consul? Sounds like you got two heads. Here's a third."

The man opened the lid of the brief-case and stuffed rolls of bills under his wife's satin *St Laurent* shirt. "Say you're pregnant! Say that it's nearly your time!" But as the woman tapped hysterically on the window, Coon heard nothing, deafening himself with an adapted refrain: "Driving this truck, high on fuck-up," and revelling in the laughter of Holy Fools.

"What would you have thought," said the cabbie, to make conversation, after a pause, "if you'd woken up this morning and known that you were going to be driven round London all day by a naked happy hyena," and then settled down into a rhetorical burble of which the words 'happy hyena', emerged and re-emerged.

"I am not interested in your observations," said the man, "what are *you* doing here anyway?"

The cab driver flipped them his cab licence in front of their livid dials, and they held their heads in their hands.

In Baker Street the cab ran into a jam. The Paraguayan looked expectant, saw a policeman catatonically high on lead fumes, but still gesticulating, trying to make sense of it all, and he gesticulated back wildly, involuntarily high on cally griff.

The jam was a Gordian knot. People started getting out of their cars, and ranting at each other, each one proclaiming the importance of their various missions, and then trying to impress it upon the catatonic bluebottle. The policeman, with the two or three brain-cells left unintoxicated, decided that the best technique was some form of displacement activity, and his eyes were soon drawn to Coon's cab. Some eidetic memory that had miraculously lingered in the sieve above his shoulders from his days at Hendon police college clicked with the behaviour that he'd just observed within the passenger compartment, and he shouted "STOP" at the top of his voice.

"Are you on duty?" said Coon, throwing him a third of a glance, "Or are you just some cardboard cut-out for a beach photographer? This 'Stop' is a Stop thirty cars deep."

"GET OUT!"

"Sure," said Coon, "hold this, passing him the jay. A

well-timed toke is better than a pig in a poke." And opened the cab door.

"What is this? What the bloody hell are you doing? Show me your licence!"

"Don't you use language to me, bitch," said Coon, towering above him. "There's only dried blood in hell, and you need a forked cock as well as a forked tongue to get in."

The policeman found himself drawn into staring at Coon's midriff like a nosey schoolboy, and then pulled out his notebook. Coon blinked, projected a five-dee photograph of Miss Tresses against his eyelids, joining together all the phosphenes with his laser pupils into a cunt-lap cornucopia, and built himself up a giant erection knocking the policeman's notebook into the air.

"There is no end to the production of books," he said, quoting *Revelation*.

The crowd was silent, but half of them still sneakingly looking at the policeman for salvation, as if his uniform was a congealed carapace of orgone energy, as if he was still the governing street guru.

Coon pulled a tag out of the policeman's pocket, wrote on it *Exhibit One*, tied it round the still massive joint, and plunged it into the policeman's mouth. The crowd were dazed and amazed. High on hard-won approval, Coon moved the street further down the road, but not before he had passed the policeman around the circle of drivers and passengers, humming in Spanish for the benefit of the Paraguayan diplomat still locked in the back: "*La Mierda al Izquierda*. Shit goes to the left and port to the right . . . Our next port is the Zoo!"

The black dragon of asphalt encrusted with starry-eyed drivers, passengers and pedestrians caught crossing the street, arrived at Regent's Park. Outside the Zoo, Coon stood on top of the cab and made a speech.

He illuminated, elevated and strengthened the crowd with such observations as : "Life on this planet started four billion years ago, and there are now four billion of us alive," which seemed to give them coincidental lock-jaw, and then finished by saying: "Where we are now, the Zoo, is a forced breeding camp for political prisoners. Our ancestors."

Coon then showered money from the Paraguayan brief-case at the Entrance clerks and led the crowd to the Ape House. "Just because Charles Darwin's parents were apes," he continued, "is no reflection on the ape. It is a very special gentleman. Now, who amongst you could fuck for twenty-four hours as toads do? Shall we go adjourn to the reptile house?"

"NO!" shouted the crowd. "Release the apes!"

Coon flipped the locks, and the Bandar-Log with fluorescent bums lived again, and then he moved towards Guy's cage, and flipped the spud-catch. "Greetings, Earth Angel. We are all one flesh," and they embraced, and then Guy the Gorilla cuddled the crowd.

"Where would you like to go, Guy?" said Coon, leaving the Paraguayans locked up in Guy's cage, almost as an afterthought (and the racoons' liberation went without saying).

Guy pointed West.

"Let us proceed on a giant loon," said Coon, and while the cabbie was giving the children rides on any animal they pointed to, boas and alligators notwithstanding, they made their escape.

"Wardour Street," said Coon. "I understand they're remaking King Kong."

"Who have they got to play the part?"

"A piece of animated polystyrene," said Coon.

"Is that good enough?"

"Ooogah boogah," said Coon.

The doorman at United Artists' Studios in Wardour Street was, to phrase a coin, uptight.

"Please do not try and ingratiate yourself with us by infecting yourself with the lowest common denominator of your employers' characteristics," said Guy. "Lead us to the Kike Ko-Op."

In the Penthouse suite, Guy suborned the assembled company with various philosophical statements and then said: "I understand that you are about to fritter away the assets of your countrymen on a fraudulent film about one of the heroes of my race. King Kong."

Dust on the boardroom table gelled like smegma. Eyes picked each other like cocktail sticks, and one man went mad, his gestures becoming automatised like a robot.

"The outside world is a golem ghetto,' said Coon.

"Am I frightening you?" said Guy. "Fear leads to gangrene. Have a slither of almond ice-cream."

Coon assisted in the materialisation. They left the room filled with it, and Guy somewhat predictably laid waste to the building. The *Evening Standard* headlines read: 'Anti-Semitic Gorilla Freezes Universal's Assets'.

It was later discovered, before the whole building caught fire, that many cans of celluloid in United Artists' basement, which showed examples of speciesism had spontaneously combusted.

"People are the only media," said Coon.

"And beasts," said Guy.

"Natch."

The streets of Soho were filled with melted ice-cream, which gave visitors the impression that they might not merely be robbed on visiting the sex-shops, clip-joints and cathouses of the vicinity, but also milked of all the juices they might ever produce.

Guy expressed a desire to return to his native soil, and therefore Coon bought him a pound-stretcher to Johannesburg, and issued him with an AKA, and an armalite sub-machine-gun, and several grenades to avoid his recapture and return to the Beasts' Belsen, and suggested to Guy that he launched a cascade of bank-notes with silver linings at the embarkation point in order to ensure the confusion of any metal-detectors, and suggested that he constantly fed money sandwiches to the keepers at the front of the flying zoo in order to have a safe journey.

They kissed each other good-bye, and a reporter, who'd already written the story in his mind: 'Guy the Gay Gorilla departs for his *alma mater* leaving in his wake a trail of etcetera etcetera,' approached Coon for a comment. "All but the soul is dust," said Coon, walking away and laughing to himself. "Let's see that as a headline."

Coon was always armed.

Armed against the media by being able to solarise or expose any film in anyone's camera with a sesame wink, so that the Gorilla story had to be entirely re-set when the lith-film had gone through the plate-makers' department totally blank.

"We are the only media," mysteriously found its way into the world's press as the caption to a blank page.

Coon rested under a tree in Hyde Park with a mild attack of outrage overload.

He rested and slept.

"King Coon, you gonna get your come-uppance soon!" he heard it in his inner ear, and composed a descant to it with a full orchestra, then he woke up and heard Miss Tresses singing it while flying a kite near the Serpentine, a kite the strings of which was studded with razor blades that was severing Zammos, Nip Specials and Two-String Perfects, and turning the tree above him into a kite graveyard.

He went over to her. She continued tugging at the kite string.

"Don't you see me? I'm impersonating the Invisible Man."

She laughed, let go the kite string, and climbed the tree with him, where they made it and everything else that goes with it, being confused by Mr and Mrs Super the Semi-Detached Suburbans strolling their Sealyhams, for woodpeckers.

Miss Tresses then descended.

"Have some manna from earth," she said, throwing him up some oranges. "What else did you do today?"

"Achieved a few small advances for Aristocrats Lib. Jah magic do."

Later that night she phoned a complex pattern of room numbers in the Dorchester Hotel, asking them to turn their lights either on or off, announcing that there was an electrical fault, until they spelt, GOOD NIGHT ASTRAL STREAKER, a hundred yards from Coon's treehouse built of Rasta Vibration.

JIMI HENDRIX

A Posthumous Interview
LESTER BANGS

Jimi, you used to sing a lot about astral planes, the cosmos and such when you were on earth. Now that you're out here, how does it stack up against what you originally envisioned?

Well, I'll tell ya. It's not like the advertisements. (*Laughs*) But then, neither was I. Because see, a lot of people got the wrong idea about me.

Like who?

Me, for starters. I didn't know what I was doing, except I dug R&B and Dylan, and found out howta get all these weird sounds outa my axe. That's where things got confused, just a little bit. Like I'm jammin' my ass off one night onstage at the Fillmore, playin' some kinda dirt bike ride round the rings of Saturn, and I look out at the crowd and they're like one big pinball machine I'm lighting up, making 'em go buzz and tilt by playing "See See Rider" backwards or something I didn't know because my fingers were turning into celery stalks and I'm afraid to look at *that*, so I shut my eyes a second but there was some kinda Marvel Comic S&M Thor's Mistress flashing this whip and snorting at me in *there* so I open 'em up again fast as I can and now everybody in the audience is Bob Denver.

What? What do you mean?

I mean that every face out there looked identical, like Bob Denver on *Gilligan's Island*, with the little hat and the ratty shirt and everything, and they were all staring up at me with that goofy Gilligans look like "What're we supposed to do now?" so I screamed out right in the middle of a chorus of another song I'd forgot anyway *"I'm the Skipper and I want you to go get Marianne and bring her here to me! I want that bitch on her KNEES!"* It seemed to make sense in the context of the lyrics at the time.

Well, it was a time of great experiment and innovation, after all.

I know I changed some things, not nearly as much as some people seem to give me credit for, but I coulda really CHANGED things. I think, if I knew then what I know now. But at the time the alternative was so irresistibly tempting, and I was tellin' ya about, screamin' my lungs out at Gilligan, I had no idea in hell what Noel and Mitch were doing, they coulda been on a Greyhound to Tucson, Arizona for all I knew or cared. So I just tore up into a long high note, held it, tore it off and decided to get the hell out of there.

Now, no sooner do I get off the stage than who do I practically slam foreheads with but Bill Graham. Asshole's been standin' there on the side of the stage watchin' me this whole time. Now he just blocks my way, grabs my arm, stares deep into my eyes and says: "Jimi. Why do you go out and play shit like that, when we both know you're capable of some of the best blues I've ever heard in my life, man."

Well, I hate to say it, but I just niggered out, played even more spaced than I was, because I didn't wanna hassle with the cat, I just wanted outa there. But if I'd been physically and psychologically capable of staying, man. I woulda said: "Because there are times when I

strongly suspect, deep down inside that *I hate the fuckin'
blues*. Every broke-down nigger behind a mule he don't
own can sing the blues. I only do blues because it's fun
and easy to get into once in a while, and because I know
all them ofays don't think a music show by a black person
is their money's worth unless they get to hear some."

*Yeah, but what about cuts like "Red House" and
"Voodoo Chile?" They were incredible songs, fantastically
played!*

They weren't exactly what you would call original com-
positions. They were good takes, especially the second
"Voodoo Chile". The long version had a nice feel, but it
was there to fill out a double album, and Winwood played
the same damn solo he played in "Pearly Queen" and
every other damn session he did for about three years. I
played good blues on "Red House", but it got way more
attention than it deserved, probably because it was so hard
to get in America for a long time. I mean, "I Don't Live
Today" is *real* blues, modern blues – it's what happens
when you drop a hydrogen bomb on the blues, which is
what it deserves.

   Listen. The blues is white music, and so was most 'free
jazz'. All the musicians know it, everybody in the ghetto
knows it because they be boppin' to James Brown and
Stanley Turrentine, don't own Muddy Waters albums
much less Robert Johnson, and 98% of 'em never *heard* of
Albert Ayler. My music was at least 70% white. If I'd
played what black people wanted to hear at that time I'da
been spectacularly unsuccessful in the hip rock superstar
world, and if I'd gone down to the Apollo Theatre and
played what I played at the Fillmore I probably woulda
been laughed off the stage. And knowing that has dogged
my ass all the way to this moment. That and the fact that
to a certain extent and in the interests of image, I had to
shuck and jive because you know niggers is just s'posed to
be *bad* and screw good wid big dicks an' be finger poppin'

all de time. I just added a little acid and feedback. And hell, for all of that I didn't even get laid that much either, or at least not as much as I should. I mean, you would think with me bein' JIMI HENDRIX and all the big deal was made out of it, I'D BE GETTIN' MORE PUSSY THAN Haile Selassie's whole harem and better quality than, I dunno, who's the hottest screw you can think of?

Uhmmmm . . . Wilma Flintstone.

Thanks a lot. Like, I coulda dug gettin' into some'a that Julie Christie, you know, or maybe some a that Ursula Andress, you know *movie stars,* continental flash class pussy. Instead I get all these dopey bitches wanna read my Tarot and always gotta I Ching in the Bantam edition in their back jeans pocket ready to spring on you at any second and tell you just the exact state of the gobbledegook. Well, I got more gobbledegook than I know what to do with already, as even a passing listen at my songs will tell you. You think I wrote all them fuckin' cosmic lyrics because I had the Universal Mind on tap? Hunh. I liked *Star Trek* but I ain't Paul Kantner. I got *more* out of it than Paul Kantner, who shoulda profited by my bad example. I just dropped this and snorted that, and pretty soon a lotta shit was swirling around my head. Same shit as hit everybody else, really, especially Dylan, who was as inspiring and as bad an influence on me as anybody. I started out sincere, but half the time I couldn't fuckin' think straight, so stuff I *knew* was sloppy-ass jive time mumbo-jumbo come tumblin' out, and people jump up like whores for a blow of coke: "Oh wow, Jimi, far out . . ." And maybe that's where things started to really go wrong, when I saw that folks'd buy that jive as profound, well, I just spaced it all a-way.

Are you saying you were a suicide?

I ain't saying nothing, man. Except maybe that no dead niggers are suicides. But it's got nothing to do with me now. 'Cause there ain't no race bullshit Out Here. Ain't no races – "Just us angels up heah, boss!" Maybe I'll come back – just once – and do a three night stint of *God's Trombones as a rock opera*, with Gil Scott-Heron and Stevie too. 'Cause I wanna lay some shit on Stevie – that cat is *off* and I don't care if he's blind, I don't care if his mama sent him to seven churches for each day of the week, he is flat *wrong*, period. I mean, nobody should know this 'Heaven' shit better'n me. I allow myself as something of an expert on the subject. It's been nothin' but blowjobs 'n' soma since I bailed out back in '70. Don't *ever* go ta Heaven, man. It's the *shits*. Only reason not to split is Hell is worse, we went down there one weekend on a binge and it's the dregs. Heaven is like total stardom with a constant-touring clause, nothin' but arenas and hotels, but Hell is like Baltimore. The whole Afterlife trip is rigged to the rim jobs, and like New York cabaret cards it's one system you can't beat.

Your rap is . . . well . . . I honestly can't think of another question right now.

That's okay, I'm on speed, I'll fill in. (*Lights a cigarette, with compulsive urgency but steady hands.*)

I get a feeling you're pretty critical of your fellow musicians, dead and living.

Yeah, but it's cool, see, because there's nobody I'm more ruthlessly critical of than myself. I was a good guitar player, no Django but I did manage to come up with a few new riffs and a few new ideas about how to finger or get some weird noises outa the thing. But there ain't much percentage in ego-tripping when you're dead, so I gotta cop that that was about *it*. The songs I wrote that had actual melodies, that you could hum or have a real zinger cover, can be counted on the fingers of one hand. "Angel" I'm still proud of, as a *composition*, and a couple others

But the rest is mostly just metal riffs, with mostly jive lyrics that I talked instead of sang. I got a lotta credit for introducing 'advanced technology' or whatever they're callin' it these days to rock, but the thing that almost everybody missed was that once the distortion and technology became a 'required' par of the whole style and, like, institutionalised, then it was all over. Because technology is cold – so's technique, for that matter – and humans are hot. Or at least they should be. Because the emotion behind the distortion is the whole thing. And what we didn't realise was that all of us cultivating distortion so much was just digging our graves, emotionally speaking. And literally too, I guess, in some cases.

Because as time went I began to realise that what people craved was just *noise*. Now, I took a lotta care with my own albums, the first three anyway – they were very carefully produced, all that shit. They were tight. But I was beginning to really, really wonder. Because when I listen to *Are You Experienced?*, at least half of what I hear and remember is just this really crazed unhappy desperation and pissed-offness that can't make no sense out of nothing. It's there in the lyrics and in the music too. Because that was where I was at the time. When I said, "*Ain't no life nowhere*," I *meant it*! Meanwhile I'm thinking do they expect me to bring the can of lighter fluid in my pocket onstage every night? Obviously something is wrong somewhere.

Well, what was it about distortion that started bothering you so much?

Well, like Graham wants blues, so do the fans, but Graham don't want distortion and they do. He thinks that's shit, and blues is 'real'. Well, I don't know *what the fuck is* real. I never exactly did. Like, do I play two chords or three or just fuck around with tremelo and feedback and make funny noises and burn my guitar and swallow the strings and cannibalise my sidemen and they stand there alone on the stage with the buttons poppin' off my shirt like Brock Peters singing "John Henry" and "Cotton Fields" back home and a selection of word songs personally recorded on Parchman by Alan Lomax? See, it seems to me when I look back that there was something larger that I always really, really wanted to do, but I could never quite get a firm grip on it.

On one level I'm really glad I got out when I did. Because it's like Kennedy see, a legend – everybody can sit around saying, "Well, gee, nothin' happenin', but if *Jimi* was around now, *he'd* show us where it was all goin' next!" But they're wrong. I wouldn't have a fuckin' *clue* what to do now, if I was so unfortunate as to be 'around'. I'd probably be just like the rest of 'em, repeating my same shit over and over until everybody is as bored as I am and we mutually agree to call it quits and I'll go sit in the islands and listen to reggae or something. Or maybe, what would be even worse, I'd be one of the ones that keeps grinding out the same old shit and *doesn't know it*: "Yeah, Jimi, your new album *Toe Jam Asteroid* is the absolute *best* thing you've done!" "Yeah, like dig, I'm hip, pops . . . just be cool." Yeah, that's how I'd cop out, come on as a real jive throwback spade wearing shades all the time, a little hat and cigarette smoke, the old Lonely Unapproachable Jazz Musician routine, sitting around in smoky clubs, sidewalk cafés, talk nothin' but bebop jive shit. "Yeah, cool, ah, that was a wiggy scene. Later." (*He breaks up laughing.*) The Thelonious Monk of the wah wah. Either that or just go hide and do session work. Become like Louie Shelton. Because I know I couldn't do what I started out to do and make it really cook.

And it ain't that I don't still got my chops. I do. Everybody's too fucking hung up on chops, though. I think the only studio album where I really burned all the way was my first one. And that's after practising night and day, year after year, trying to learn it all and do it better, coming up hard and fast and paying dues and busting your chops and out to whip ass on everybody, when suddenly one day I discovered somehow that I could be fuckin' Segovia and if that *some other weird component* is missing, then I might as well be Louie Shelton.

What is that component?

I wish I knew. I know I lost it somewhere. I take consolation in the fact that just about everybody else came up same time as I did too. Maybe we all just got too high.

How do you feel about people like Eric Burdon and Buddy Miles, whom some observers have accused of cashing in on your name or their association with you after your death?

Listen, once you kick out you tend to let a *lotta* bad shit just go under the bridge. Fuck it, I hope they copped a few extra bucks. Besides, nobody lives forever, and I'm gonna have to sit down and have a serious talk with poor old Eric whenever he gets up here, in lieu of busting his face open. It's actually amusing, and besides, he really didn't know any better. Buddy Miles is a different case – I'd be afraid of getting *my ass* kicked, but anybody racks up as many bad records at that cat's probably gonna end up on the first coal cart to Hell anyway, so hopefully I'll never chance to see his fat face again.

Ever see any of the others who kicked off close to the time you did, hanging around up here?

Nah. I *hear* about them once in awhile, but I don't hang out with 'em. You wouldn't either. Morrison – I heard all about him, although I didn't see it. He put up such a big stink how he wanted into Hell and wasn't gonna make 'em all wish he'd never died, and on and on . . .

I identify with him on a certain level we both came along at the right wrong time, right to become figureheads, wrong in terms of longevity. We were like the test models for crap like Alice Cooper and David Bowie. We both got suckered, but I like to think he got suckered far worse than I did. He, like, had more *complicity* in his own destruction. I like to think I just got more confused, and basically confused musically as much as in life, until it was all too much of a mess and there was no way out. I let too damn many people intimidate me, for one thing, because I knew *I* was off but I never had the simple street-smarts to figure just maybe *they were off* too, maybe ten thousand times worse than me, so I just kind of ended up laying myself in everybody's hands. I mean, I was really and innocent, and it wasn't comfortable then.

What about Janis?

I was hoping you weren't going to ask me that. Jeez, you fuckin' journalists, always after the next lurid headline. Well . . . she was pathetic there and she's pathetic here. It's not her fault, but she doesn't do anything, particularly, to try to improve it, either. That's all I got to say about that.

How do you feel about being a hot chart artist still, and record companies over-dubbing other accompanists on your old tapes?

My records still selling is just like Jefferson Starship being more popular then Jefferson Airplane – quality has nothing to do with it, it's just people hanging onto things they know were good and represented something *once*, instead of taking a chance on a dubious unknown artist.

As far as the over-dubbing goes, I feel almost as much indifference there. It sounds weird and egotistical for a dead guy to crow about how he was actually a one-man show, especially since his old sidemen really have no means of retorting, so obviously the smart position for me to have is no position. Why don't you go ask John Coltrane the same question, and see if connubial fidelity extends beyond the grave.

You seem pretty negative about the people who've followed you musically on earth, though.

Yeah. I am. Because they're cold. I may have played real dogshit some gigs, and cut some tracks that were too smooth for my taste. But I was loose. There was something bigger than me sweeping me along and it killed me in the end, but some pretty incredible music came out of it at times, too. My only regret is that I wonder how much of it under those circumstances, was really *my music*, when you get right down to it. If a lightning bolt strikes you, and out of it you get a masterpiece, well, is it you or the lightning bolt? And in the final analysis it's just no contest. You know you lost control, you let the music and the life play you, and that's why you went under. But it really happened, it was real fire and real dues, and nothing can erase that. It should be pretty obvious by now that I consider my life and my art a failure, but it was an honest failure.

What bugs me is these cats now – no bolt. And no them either! I don't mind people copping my riffs, but they're like a buncha college students! Most of my riffs *I* copped off somebody else, but then I went on and played and forgot about it. I didn't sit around with seven candles burning in a shrine to Chuck Berry. So who even cares if cats like this Trower or that guy in Canada succeed or fail, what's the fucking difference? There is more happening in any bar on Friday night when the dance floor's full, than in all those cats' albums and concerts put together.

What's even worse is that they missed the biggest lick of all, the thing that was so discouraging to me – that I saw the end of it coming. I don't mean rock 'n' roll or popular music or even heavy metal – just the kind of the particular experimental, technological branch we riffed out on and sawed through. There's got to be something else. Because one thing I learned while killing myself was that a hell of a lot of that shit was just sound and fury kicked

JIMI HENDRIX

EDITED BY LIPPMANN+RAU

EXPERIENCE FEAT: EIRE APPARENT

up to disguise the fact that we were losing our emotions, or at least the ability to convey them. Most of *Electric Ladyland* and the second album sound real cold to me now. I don't know what it sounded like to me then, because I was too spaced out to make any accurate judgement except that it had all the ingredients. I got some rocks off especially in things like "Voodoo Child (Slight Return)", the albums were relatively slick and I knew they would sell.

I guess that's what I was trying to get at before when I talked about the missing component. I just forgot how to feel unless I was getting electric shocks or something – and after awhile even electric shocks began to feel all the same. And even saying it like that doesn't really explain it. It's really THE great mystery, for everybody Out Here. And nobody's come up with any solid answers yet. So when you get back, when you publish this, if anybody comes up after that and tells you they got some kind of a line on it, I don't care how thin it is, well, you'd be doing me the biggest favour of my death if you'd pass it on back. I'd like that more than anything in the . . . cosmos.

(He laughed again, briefly, then stared through us into some sort of distance. It was obviously time to go.)

(Statement of fact) MERVYN FALLS TO THE GROUND.
(Question) WAS IT **MURDER?**
(SOLUTION TO PROBLEM) Let him **LIE** there.

A FORTNIGHT ON CALVARY

DON'T PUT ME DOWN LIKE ALL THE OTHER FISH

David Britton. 1st May. 1977.

PAUL BUCK

The Kiss

Violation 22

The cunt of the sexual parasite is distressed by the use of the combustible foreskin. Towards this orifice where she had become the shadow of her cold mouth she plunged his head, pressing her vulvar lips into what contained the lavish. Selecting what is contorted and pleasing I anticipate that both her legs will be gripped by his fatigued hands. The undressed body will be flagellated. Hesitation in this act drains the dominant delights from their attachments. She strains towards spending without making him discharge. But since this simple opening eliminates continuity your disgust blots fruitful connections. Confined orifices excite compulsive savagery. All equal voluptuousness disappears. Damage moves swiftly. It will droop and separate. The kind of force which encloses the fuck does not drain the fear of despair. If she had a cunt that bound me a bared passion would stick in the burst blackness. Having been praised for digging into her vagina with strength, with a prolonged and ordained humour, he is now controlled by her thrust. Crushed forbiddance pursues and screws the postures bound by romance. Towards the end of the first kiss her cunt negates all comparison with her other openings. Desire is held over the anus. It is abandoned by careful language and changes which obliterate the provocation. She does not dissuade us to combine force and inhibition and thus consume the challenge. Whoever responds to her muscularity might be received in her arms. Whoever caresses the changed movement slows the others legs which spread. She can press distortion as far as necro-cunnilingus. Bodies, activities and movements warn him to curve the nubile's back to obtain the required confinement, to elevate the obliteration of previous erections. Bound by the memory of whores and bled by their atmosphere he pulls away from the crutch that was convulsing. Nobody hits the limit. Only mistakes elevate criminality. Nubiles copulate whilst whores gobble. Satisfaction is a bound scream reversed. Wounded by mature movement and distortion she fights off the manipulation within. Draining. Beating admits an open sacrifice that monstrousness banishes by collapse. His semen satisfies the needs of the mouth. Passion is only a massive realisation that a lapse in folding can sadden availability. Holes and writhings are sacrificed by further lies. To gouge her eyes he goes beyond transgression, shooting through all that is notched. No other can writhe. I do not want to stop unless it beats capability. Bounced by bosoms. Manipulated by a female crouch. This body can be very satisfactorily excited. Her genitals and breasts though flattened by delays of boldness are finally handled by forbidden saturation. Beneath other frequented nubiles hilarity is controlled. She turns aside the wanton split that was ruled when crudeness was recalled to cunnilingus. She can still be aroused. She can turn and turn if squeezed by salacious solitude. Or debased by what is now frequently disguised as that which melts in the embrace. What they can reach together elevates contradiction.

september–october 74

Kiss Kiss

Violation 53

Tapestry of the minge. Seize the
   flourishing of the damp
   tampering. More limitations.
   Odour toughened by distorted
   cries. Theft has been
   broadened. Wedge decays and
   shifts the look. Open one
   more leg for me. Abscess
   bared. Or orifice let
   whiten. Necrophilia protects
   the tongue. Arousal bestows

a mask. She is already the
thirst. With the serration
comes the gasp. Drips. She
is what she thirsts for.

Modified wrist. Clamour and divest before
the sores of the risk. Before
noise arouses the compulsion
of the relapse. Before display
flagellates the language.

Within the coupling. Within savagery. The
scramble of sighs would force the
tapestry into a stain that limits
the oblique and forces the pubic
entrancement to double the cracks.
Penetrate silence. Pluck sudden
loose stumbles. Anus with a kiss
to deposit. The faeces of a friction moistened.

Pressure to coldness. This bondage has an
immediacy crossed by curves of the
other meditations. From this restraint
adherence replaces what the placenta
showered. The mystery inside an uprising.

What she likes about provocation hollows
failure. The subvertion of insistence.
The distortion of the surface is the
constraint to be reflected.

Within the thighs she must unfasten a
freshness astride evisceration.
Cracks stained by stakes. Discharge
between the derangement and a gasp.
Each retort is the gasp of
innocence of one who has twisted the
burns. Probability is the last of

the evasions which the thirst as
language will release as a
subversion. By thrashing us twists
reverse the torment. Lock the clasp on the cyst.

Viciousness imposes imprisonment on
delirium. A prison of lost
desires. A nourishment and that
which always inverts itself.
What is invoked by hurling the
ultimate couple itself. Moisten
the provocation of the pubis.
Of pressure intended to transfuse
the consciousness. The
question of melting pressures
the elimination of it. Receive
it. It is an immensity. Out
there begins the posture of the
halt. This immensity is my
obsession. In the genitals is
the hanged oblation. The
constraint reaps impotence.

october 75–april 76

MICHAEL BUTTERWORTH

Stick

1. An empire of natural beauty

Stick was the builder of the stairs on Cain. One point: Stick had devised them so they would collapse after the natives had climbed halfway to the top.

While work went on destroying the planet's urbanised features, I actually talked to Stick for some time. He is tiny and sharp. He is a blood corpuscle out of an elephant's bloodstream. He had his hands in his pockets, shrilling out orders to the niggers every few seconds. His voice is so tiny someone had felt is necessary to build an amplifier into his mouth. You can hear him chewing and making foul noises with his miniature teeth:

"Sex of any sort disgusts me – as soon as I get these shits under my thumb" (holding up a placard saying HUMAN RACE) "I'll stop sex altogether."

He disappeared without bothering to come back.

I could feel a small metallic rat busying on my skin, prickling in my hair, sniffing with whiskers down my ears, all places at once with the speed of a bullet. The loudspeaker system of his head drowned his tiny nervous system with pain every time he tried to speak. He picked up a placard and wrote. "I WILL – WITH THE AID OF NIGGERS – BUILD AN EMPIRE OF NATURAL BEAUTY."

His secretary, Twig, a tall thin chap with glasses – which burnt his eyes out whenever he opened them – said: "He hates cities and gods; he'll take over the universe and turn it into a paradise of flowers and birds."

2.   Meanwhile, in a distant corner of the Galaxy

". . . *somebody*, is robbing me of my PIGGY bank!

(The trees of this planet are unlike any trees in the universe.)

"SOMEbody has stolen my finger ring for attracting birds. If I don't get it back soon I'll have to go on Brylcreem for a bit."

(The attraction of the bulb flower is irresistible. Lights flash on and off in your head when you pass it.)

But as I sit at my desk – Control – reports come from all OVER the universe, and come flooding in in tidal waves:

"I've had my hair cut off."

"The Brylcreem menace has struck – what shall I do? I've tried spit but it's no so good."

"Awkward! Awkward!"

"Get this thing out of my kitchen!"

Later in the night I had a vision of teeth.
Dec. 8th. Slept well.

3.   Interview in Control Office

Stick got up in arms – became all hairy. The last bus had got home. He'd missed it.

He jumped up square into my office, face contorted in mimic of a faulty hairdryer.

The tapes recorded everything:

"The Stigma Riots have little to do with what I'm doing. They help to scare these little shits (holding up a placard of the HUMAN RACE) into believing what I believe I believe."

"Then your aim is not to convert your subjects to a proven policy, rather to a policy which you believe should be proven? When will you become a preacher of fact?"

"I will never become a preacher – least of all of a fact. What good are facts? Orders are the thing! It's all in the mind nowadays."

4. The schizophrenic theory of mind

"Any interest is interest in a component. Total interest (a simultaneous summing-up of the entirety of universal affairs) would by definition be a total physical as well as mental mergence with universal affairs and therefore would not as some people seem to think be an interest of any sort. What an impossible feat to take an interest in a complete range of possible individual interests unless the experimenter first swaps his identity with that of the universe and, through the medium of that reverse, takes interest in himself, secondly dropping dead through nervous exhaustion!"

5. Concerning the intelligence

INTERVIEWER: What is your favourite science?
STICK: Botany.
INTERVIEWER: Why?
STICK: Botany is the science of our vegetative existence and not as some intelligent people think, a study of plantlife, the habits.
INTERVIEWER: So botany is really a social science?
STICK: Not at all. Botany is the science of human vegetation. The only friend I've got in the world looks exactly like a twig.

6. Tour round the Stick laboratories

An atmosphere of soil was everywhere. Deep lifts had taken me to the back-benches of the most obscure government in the universe. The laboratories actually stank of soil chemical fumes and Stick. Large worms were strewn about on immense dissecting tables and were floodlit with powerful million-kilowatt light bulbs. Twig, myself and the Stick Boost reporter, accompanied by visitors in up-turned raincoats, dark glasses and long hair, turned out of the dissecting room and entered a long dimly lit corridor. To the right-hand head of this was a door which opened out into the development laboratories.

"Research is going on," came information from an overloud loudspeaker.

Stick was nowhere to be seen. I kept hearing him rocketing overhead at immense speeds chased by books with open arms, minutely crashing the sound barrier in explosions that shook the whole mansion.

"You are in the Development Laboratories . . ."

I had heard previously of Stick's plans to build a super race of emotionless, nerveless plantmen.

My eardrums burst. We could see two doctors and their staff clearly. Plants were everywhere. I had a mad vision of chemists asking "Why?" Why did urbanism turn into a madhouse for donkeys?

The laboratories were in a shocking state resembling chemical pigsties. Entrails, stale blood, chemicals, broken glass littered the floor. We stood on a dry island of chemical and biological refuse surrounded by a sea of poison that emitted weird flashes and sullenly fumed.

Stick was somewhere about.

We met a crowd of cardboard doctors and staff who waved their arms at us but did not speak.

7. *The pre-take-off nightmares Twig had*

Metallic bats flutter against his pointed head. Large shapes advance from the edges of a rocky horizon. On the horizon a grotesque ship made out of fishbones stands luminous.

The room is filled with elephants. They dance and fill the ship's compartments with magical droppings.

8. Speech in cold space

"For convenience I have divided the universe into four sectors or systems. As you know, the universe consists of solid masses which generally aggravate the ether. The universe is infinite YET IT IS bounded!

"Like everything else the universe has its cancers. I heave already mentioned aggravation of the ether by a solid, which aggravates Time by aggravating itself via the webs of the ether; itself is responsible for Time – matter measures time."

Stick paused after sipping coffee, then emotion suddenly welled up.

"May the . . . I mean I would like to say that I AM NOBODY'S PISSOIR!"

9. The sounds of space

Space plants: these things don't pretend to cry. They do cry. I've heard them wailing as they've floated past, tears on to earth, spacemen with fins flicking about in the ether living among splendid foliage of space and crusted with red. But they are harsh plants, spiky, not to be touched, suggestive of a bad dream. I have called them dream-plants.

CONTROL: I am losing control. This morning I can't remember whether I had a chat with Stick last night or not. He seems to be everywhere at once. Stick is closing in.

Aug. 3rd. Slept badly.

A peculiar flower on Lostar (famous for its orchids) has spread planetwide, choking the orchids. It has metal ovaries.

10. Finale

"Oh please oh PLEASE come back, Stick," wrote a lady

in high hat and dress. "I love you *too* much for you to go.
"I love you."

And indeed, people on earth were loving Stick everywhere. In fact the one person Stick couldn't stand loved
him too much most:

"*God* loves you most. Come back, son," a father said,
holding up a placard saying MEET THY DOOM – THE
END IS AT FINGER.

And in short, spangled earth had lost its god for the
time being, and if its people cried it was because they
weren't use to being without a god.

People rioted. They grew hair down to their knees and
raped one another. The thing was, earth never *had* had it
so good or so bad at the same time.

The Pub That Exploded

Mercer smiled to himself as he walked over to his wife's
grave. His only object was to laugh himself under with
her. For a while he strode in circles round the graves kicking at the headstones mad searching for something.

Mercer took in the bar at a glance. It was long and
stretched to feed trash to a large catmouth in the distance.
Several characters littered the floor. An old sailor sucked
his dog's prick.

In a corner sat a middle-aged businessman drinking
water from a fountain. After exercising his muscles on a
trapeze the businessman turned away to look out of a
window, then carried on with his drink.

On top of a chair an old woman stood drinking gin
and peeling the skin off large round limes.

Offering him butter from a butterdish a sexy girl tried to put her brown arms into his slim pockets. He stepped over her roughly and ground her face into the fresh paint.

A leather youth snaked out from under a chair.

The barman found a tap and squirted beer over the ceiling. A woman screamed with pleasure.

The floor turned red.

The cat never lowered its head. Its white milkline grew on the bartop horizon, white trash at a hundred miles an hour. Liquid, repulsive.

His drink in one hand, a drink in another, Mercer tried to walk to the nearest table. The youth started. Glass splinters shone out of his eyes. One by one the squares to Mercer grew less. Attached to a bony hand a flicked blade screwed up into the air. Mercer sat up screaming. Eyes turned to him. Drinks were dropped.

She wore no pants.

The old sailor spun out of his clothes.

The floor cracked down the centre.

The sexy girl split open her face. Red hair streamed up from the crack into the beer air.

The white milkline spread white blotches in front of his eyes. Waves buffeted out of the ceiling stroking his hair. Whiteness engulfed him. A sick terror feeling glued his legs together at the tops.

One after another.

The cat let out a scream of success, chased its tail madly for a few seconds and arched its back.

The barman –

The youth –

The sex girl –

The old woman –

The old sailor –

His dog –

The walls danced. The sky fell in. Grey cloud bolted down in fantastic knots from the sky. Wet greenery thrust tendrils through the wooden blooden floor.

His feet crashed on to the heavy porch. Mercer

trembled. He snatched at the carrotman's wristwatch and ran off with it, ticking. At a safe distance he turned round to face the pub. He wound the watch till its springs broke. He filled it with dead leaves and hurled it backwards towards the pub.

Flash.

The pub exploded.

Mercer crawled out of the broken wreckage of the church feeling for his hands. His face smarted. Fire-burning air poured out of the deadstone trees stooped like road lamps over the graves. Under a sodium conifer tree he sat down to cry, breaking his toes on the hard ground.

He sat upon her grave. He cried again and slept out in the stars dreaming of summer.

SUMMER we have summer in our veins, the leaves of the conifer tree died saying: SUMMER we have summer in our veins.

The conifer tree began to tingle.

Sing sing, called voices to him from across the water.

"I have just blown up a pub. I have killed some people. Oh I got to rely on God."

On the other side of him raged war.

"I don't care," Mercer said after a while. "I don't care." Where are the other voices?

"Where are the other voices?"

The conifer tree rustled a secret, then was silent. The cloudworld vanished. Severed wrists fell down from the sky and hung in front of his blue eyes on the ends of puppet strings. Streaked across with barbed wire.

The ruined church coughed in the loud night and was silent.

In Mercer's other world the pub blew up in spurts people on to planets and strange characters into back gardens.

The trees dripped hot splats of solder on to the graves matching the tinsel of his hair.

His wife's dead hand closed over his own and drew

85

him down into the cold water. He whimpered.

From somewhere, the voices started up.

". . . mad have . . . now we know . . . never oit yui."

"Will you wake up?"

"Will you wake up?"

A thunderbolt. Mercer felt hot fire coursing down his cheeks. Limbs of shadow crisscrossed his eyes and shifted some pink cloud, veined red into the interior of his skull. The comet burst, scattering painful red.

"Have you gone mad?" A blue-green face peered into his own.

"Who is it? Who is it?"

Holly leaves rustled somewhere. Particles of soil shifted before his gaze.

The blue-green face peered down.

Mercer coughed. His gaze followed a long thin arm into the clouds, losing sight of anything.

Two characters were sitting on a bench. They came over.

"Will you tell me what happened?" Mercer stood up. Cloud obscured the horizon.

"She's over there."

Mercer stared into the cloud.

"We saw you grab her tits off!"

Mercer tried to walk slowly towards his wife.

He sidestepped a shower of burning fall-out.

"You tried to tread on her face!" an excitable male said.

She had her back to him. Tracerlike objects began to come up in the air from behind him, slowly and then more rapidly as they turned into boxes of matches piling in piles at her feet.

"Listen to me," he called her. "Whatever I said I meant nothing."

Believe me, the conifers whispered.

His feet crunched on the dry twig ground. But already the matches were flowering into tall grasses with heads of cold flame that swayed before her face.

86

Mercer turned to face the two men. His vision returned to normal. They traipsed off into the trees.

On the wind he could still hear their laughter, coming from the pub across the road.

Mr Bloody Blue-green face, Mr Bloody Excitable Man.

It came to Mercer he had seen the two men before, sometime in the short interval.

He shuddered in the cold wind.

Gravediggers!

The moon came out.

He heard their last laughter.

The ground was churned up. A few empty bottles littered the ground by the foot of her grave and sandwich papers and cigarette ends filled up the gaps in his head.

A cigar length away the white softness of the pub exploded again, mushrooming into something unpleasant.

His aching brain.

PAUL ABLEMAN

Nick

Nick S. was a passenger on the big jet that ripped through a forest near Paris recently. After the crash ribbons of fabric and flesh dripped from miles of ravaged trees. Few of the bodies could be assembled into recognisable wholes and there were no survivors.

I hardly knew Nick and yet my memories of him dive back through the years. I see him, drunk and morose, amidst the flickering revelry of the old Boite club in Soho, and that's been closed for fifteen years. 'Decadent' was a word that often seemed to occur to people when they contemplated Nick and he was certainly no Boy Scout. I remember meeting him in Soho more than a decade ago and asking conventionally:

"All right?"

"Hm?"

His patronising manner instantly transformed me, on a mental monitor screen, into a provincial. Normally we ignored each other but there were few customers in the bar and, our eyes having met, I'd felt that some acknowledgement was unavoidable. Now I was reproaching myself for not having snubbed him when, abruptly, he smiled and his sullen, exquisite features shone with grace. He confided:

"I can hardly stand. I've been at it all day."

Despondently I inferred what he'd been 'at', something his slender form, raven hair and pale, eerily-perfect features made readily available to him. I knew his account would choke me with envy but there was no escaping it.

So I grinned fixedly as he chattered on about his

'amazing' sculptor-friend who'd asked him that morning if he 'felt like a scene' and about the three 'birds' who'd come fluttering round to the 'incredible' studio and about the wondrous things they'd all done together on the sculptor's 'fantastic' bed. Immediately he'd finished, and while I was still chuckling and nodding, boredom reclaimed his expression and he glanced about for better company.

In the skirmishes between us, he wielded the delicate blade of beauty and then retired into the citadel of social success. Mounted on my clumsy steed of integrity, I whirled my mace of culture ferociously but never connected. The origin of this saloon-bar joust was a forgotten innuendo, his or mine, that had stung and conditioned all our future meetings.

But there came an evening, four or five years later, when it seemed that an armistice might be signed. It happened on my territory, in the saloon of the Musketeer. Spangled with dying snowflakes, I shouldered my way into the mellow room, and as I hung up my dripping donkey-jacket, heard the peevish but peremptory voice:

"I want a bloody drink!"

The barman's reply was inaudible but could be inferred from the other's invitation to:

"Then call the bloody police!"

Was it Nick? The voice seemed congruous with his remembered one but he'd never, to my knowledge, been in this pub before. I hung up my coat slowly considering whether it might not be wiser to put it on again and depart. Nick could be exceedingly tiresome. Then a sense of the ignominy of being chased from my own local decided me. I flicked the loop over the hook and turned. The saloon was thronged and I couldn't locate him at first. I worked my way towards the bar and had nearly achieved it when, in profile, I glimpsed his pale scowl. His collar was open and soiled and his cheek was stubbled but he was still insolently handsome. I was contemplating him with mixed dislike and admiration when he glanced round, saw me and conceded recognition with a curt nod.

Flushing at having been once again wrong-footed by him, I returned the nod and edged closer. I asked:

"What's up?"

"These bloody idiots won't give me a drink."

Although reluctant to ratify his classification, I glanced questioningly at Fred, the barman, who shook his head.

"Why not?" I asked.

"He's barred – s'all I know."

An unexpected urge to take Nick's side gripped me. After all, we were veterans, he and I, of madder evenings in wilder places. Hadn't we capered together in the legendary Boîte? When Jack, the manager, came frowning up to support Fred, I argued Nick's case vehemently. Confident that I was a valued customer, I felt sure Jack would yield. It seemed to me important to demonstrate to Nick how much pull I had in this place. But Jack was stupidly adamant. Nick was not going to be served. I shrugged bitterly and suggested to Nick that we sit down. When he seemed reluctant, I jabbed my finger covertly towards my own glass to indicate that we could share it. He seemed to understand but, once we were seated, merely sat and morosely chewed his nails. Somehow I interpreted this as gratitude for my efforts and became expansive. I myself had recently been banned from a hole called The Galleon. Did Nick know it? He shook his head faintly and I accepted this as a sign that comradeship was sprouting. I suggested we adjourn to more hospitable premises. But he didn't seem to grasp my meaning and, in a little while, stood up and, with a sour look at the barman, departed. I was a shade offended by his coolness but nevertheless felt that I had, with great diplomatic skill, saved the situation.

I was still indulging in mild self-congratulations when, with an amazing crash, an empty bottle hurtled through the frosted-glass window and struck a lady on the shoulder. She gave an indignant cry. There were gasps and shouts and the manager charged round the bar and out into the narrow street. A number of excited youths followed him. I didn't. I sat and nursed my fury. The bastard! The decadent, violent bastard! Shards from the great sheet of glass might have slashed someone badly. The spoiled, vicious, narcissistic brat!

But the next time we met it was quite different. Several more years had passed and I was spending a few days in a provincial city. Crossing the lobby of my hotel one evening I found that the spruce, springy man approaching from the revolving door was offering me a warm smile. Certainly there was something vaguely familiar about the fellow but, so radical was the change, that Nick was wringing my hand before I'd found a name and a history for him.

I was on my way to an appointment but that evening we met by arrangement in the bar. He was cordial, poised and courteous. He told me that he taught three days a week at the local art school. He enthused about the design of the new city centre. He mentioned a project that his class had done for the local gas-board. I found it a trifle surreal, like listening to Napoleon extolling pacifism or Lenin preaching bourgeois virtues.

Somewhat maliciously, I asked:

"How did you make out?"

"Make out?"

"With the fuzz?"

I was referring to the fact that, as I'd subsequently heard, after smashing the window of The Musketeer he'd backed away down narrow Bottle Street almost into the arms of two policemen.

"Oh you mean – "

He grimaced as if at the memory of some deprecable, but in a way endearing, pecadillo. He offered:

"Bloody silly. My wife – "

The word astonished me. I'd seen Nick with dozens of girls, many of them obviously infatuated with him, but never one that seemed permanent. However, before he could amplify further, something attracted his attention and he raised a hand in salute. I glanced in the appropriate direction and saw, flitting shyly about the lobby, a dainty thing in a tiny skirt. He explained:

"One of my students. She's got a problem."

He stood up. It was clear that he felt an obligation to go and search for solutions. I said:

"Perhaps I'll see you at breakfast."

"What? Oh no, I don't stay here."

"Really?"

"Just use it as a base. But I'll probably be in the bar same time tomorrow."

He wasn't in the bar the following evening and the next morning I drove back to London. And I can't be sure if, over the next few years I ever did see him again. My memory sometimes suggests the image of his pale face and raven hair bobbing across a bar-room but I may be transposing it from an earlier occasion. I am certain, however, that I never spoke to him again. Then, the other day, I heard that he'd been on that fatal DC-10.

Do you recall the incident? The cargo-hold door had been carelessly bolted and, in the opinion of most investigators had been blown outwards at altitude by air pressure within the plane. As a result, the cabin floor had collapsed, severing the main control cables. The desperate pilot had succeeded in levelling the dive and the huge plane had finally skimmed into a forest, shearing off miles of tree-tops and progressively disintegrating.

It plucks at the imagination. Even without personal involvement, you can't help wondering: how was it? How was it when the great machine, serene above the clouds, first cracked and shuddered? But I can't help also speculating: how was it for Nick? Did he join in the chorus of gasps and cries, leap to his feet and mill with those struggling in the aisles? Or would it have been more in character for him to clench his fists and sit very still? Was he one of those whirled into space on jets of outrushing air? Or did he ride the stricken hull as it staggered in the sky and then settled into its long death-glide to earth.

There must have been people – his mother perhaps, or possibly that improbable wife – for whom Nick was a continuous being, with stable qualities. But for me he was a recurrent engima, a gem of many facets, an intermittent man. And perhaps that idea expresses some essential truth about us all in the world of atoms and engines. Since we can now dart around the earth like dragonflies about a pond, possibly the glint of a wing and a brief arabesque is all we can reasonably expect from each other. And when the stupendous machines that sustain this airy dance fail, why then we tend to die as we have lived; in fragments.

RICHARD KOSTELANETZ

Milestones in a Life

A Fictional Narrative

0	Birth
1	Teeth
2	Walk
3	Talk
4	Read
5	School
6	Toys
7	Television
8	Games
9	Swim
10	Hobbies
11	Books
12	Baseball
13	Football
14	Friends
15	Girls
16	Smoking
17	Sex
18	College
19	Fraternising
20	Copulation
21	Study
22	Commencement
23	Military

24	Marriage
25	Job
26	Daughter
27	Promotion
28	Son
29	Responsibility
30	Exhaustion
31	New Job
32	Failure
33	Unemployment
34	Divorce
35	Indolence
36	Loneliness
37	Remarriage
38	Extravagance
39	Indebtedness
40	Raise
41	Daughter
42	Perseverance
43	Vice-Presidency
44	Speculations
45	New House
46	Cadillac
47	Son
48	Country Cottage
49	Over-Extensions
50	Collapse
51	Separation
52	Psychoanalysis
53	Reconciliation
54	Grandchild
55	Prosperity
56	Drinking
57	New House
58	Private Schooling
59	Illness
60	Recuperation
61	Leadership

J. JEFF JONES

Howl Now

for Bob, John, Paul, Joni, Eric, Frank . . . and on and on and on.

I saw the best minds of my generation destroyed by
                                                    success,
flatulent smug fashionable,
chauffered through the neon avenues at sunset looking for
where it's at
prettyfaced celebrities hungry for the latest admiration
                                            connection
with the starmaking media lens in the machinery of fame,
who wealthy and velvetwrapped and buttercheeked and
                                                    groovy
sat up toking in the jaded indirect lighting
of Laurel Canyon haciendas
floating across heated swimming pools contemplating
                                                    contracts,
who bared their assholes to agents under silk sheets and
                                                        saw
gangraped groupies writhing on penthouse floors
dimwitted,
who passed through festivals with dull pinpoint eyes
                                                    deluded
about their chemically exaggerated wisdom and self-
                                    indulgent wastefulness,
who were expelled from Holiday Inns for uninspired
                                                    vandalism

and scrawling dull graffitti on the screens of the colour
TVs,

who cowered in recording studios in naked fear
burning the company's money
as squandered talent finally ran out
and listening to the Terror through the wall
as obscurity came to get them forever . . .

THE
BRIAN ALDISS
INTERVIEW

Charles Partington
David Britton

REPORT ON PROBABILITY A is now one of the few
novels I can enter at will, and still like and feel for. It
seems to me that a lot of writers pursue in their lives
precisely the sort of repetition that I've built into it. It's a
tricky sort of thing playing with boredom. How far can
you go? How far dare you bore the reader to show him
what everyday life is like? And science fiction readers in
particular want to escape into those lovely, gaudy
universes, right? E. E. Smith and all that. REPORT is the
anti-E. E. Smith novel if you like, where life in the novel
is just about as drab and repetitive and mysterious as it is
in real life. That is what I was trying to do.

*How did you feel about reaction from the fans to that
novel, because it wasn't very well received was it?*

Oh, fans are very kind; but although they are only a tiny
part of the readership they don't come up and say, except
for the psychotics, "Brian that was a fucking awful
novel." They just don't mention it. And perhaps after a
year or two they read it again and see there was some

merit in it after all. And then they are very generous. They come up and say, "Just read PROBABILITY A again, and you know, it isn't half as bad as I thought it was."

I remember that happening with THE DARK LIGHT YEARS. A lot of people read that book and their initial reaction was one of, well not disgust, but unease. Then when I spoke to several fans later on about it, some months later, when they had re-read it, they found it significant.

I don't build my books like a lot of other science fiction writers. In THE DARK LIGHT YEARS, you've probably heard me say this, what made me write it was a burst of anger against Dr John Lilly and his horrible book on dolphins. His assumption was that dolphins are almost as intelligent as man, maybe as intelligent, so we must communicate. Now, how do we do it? We saw a hole in their skulls and sink electrodes in their brains. The worst side of the scientific method. What a way to try and proceed! It's the sort of thing he'd do with blacks if he could get them. It's such a degrading thing. Since then, Lilly has changed his approach to life.

(At this point the telephone rings. Brian has been asked to appear on the David Frost Show, due to be shown live the following day, Sunday. What follows is Brian's answers to the show's organiser. We found it amusing . . .)

"Oh, what now? Hello. Yes, well I drove up from Southmoor and in fact it took me five hours, and I was pushing hard in a Volvo. I don't know what they've got locally but maybe they wouldn't do it any faster. It looks simple enough on a map but it's a very long way . . . How much hair did he tear out? Good. You haven't thought of asking my friend Kingsley Amis, I suppose? Yes. Yes. Oh, well he's at some celebrity's do. Ask me some other time. Yes . . . C. S. Lewis is dead. Yes, some other time."

To hell with it. Now, where was I? Oh yes, the point I wanted to make about DARK LIGHT YEARS was this. I'd read another book, a book called MADKIND, a profound and mad thing by a man called Berg. And it seemed to me that his thesis that mankind was mad, that the whole species had somehow got a twist, was proved by this cruel nonsense about dolphins. So this I put in the book. But there's only one place where I state the theme in so many words. The whole novel is built around that theme. But instead of saying it all the time I only say it once and then the speech goes to a character called Mrs Warhoon. She suddenly says, "Well, mankind's mad. The reason that you don't like the Utods is because their way of life is different, they wallow in their own dung. But that's all right. That's their way. Mankind had separated himself from all basic natural things, and is so obsessed with plumbing that he has lost his natural life." And instantly all the other characters turn round and destroy her and say, "Oh piss off. Come off this coprophiliac kick! Forget about it. Now come on, talk sense." And that's all. So on the surface it might appear I'm for these horrible ideas. But you know in real life the true viewpoint is often argued out of court like that. Nevertheless it survives. That's what happens in THE DARK LIGHT YEARS. People read it and long afterwards the truth dawns. "Aldiss isn't just being horrible, he's on the side of light and goodness!" Writing in this oblique method is partly a reaction against all the diagramatic science fiction. You know – where there's an idea or thesis to prove, and the writer begins and ends with that thesis and the whole story's so built around one idea that real life doesn't enter into it. If you read Shakespeare's plays – take ROMEO AND JULIET, a nurse comes in and has a tiny part to play. But she enters talking about something else before she gets down to activating that bit of plot. Thus Shakespeare sets a sense of reality creeping in. Because that's how people are. They've got something they primarily want to do – seduce a girl let's say – but nevertheless they're turning around signing a contract or having another drink. Your mind's on more than one thing; This is the method that I try to employ in my books.

You mentioned starting a novel, the way you planned or didn't plan THE DARK LIGHT YEARS. Do you work from a tight plot, or do you tend to evolve it as you go along?

I write a lot of notes, but that's the painful bit – getting it right first of all. I think methods vary from book to book. I was so angry when starting THE DARK LIGHT YEARS that the idea was sufficient to throw me right into the book and carry me all the way through. This was when I was living in the centre of Oxford. There was a fan group there, the Speculative Fiction Group, and they were always coming around. I shut them out for a month, shut everyone out and just went ahead and fired that book off. I generally write slowly, but in this case I knew exactly what I wanted to do and went ahead and did it.

You say that you normally write slowly, but in your autobiographical work, THE SHAPE OF FURTHER THINGS you state that you sat down and wrote it in a fever, working till all hours. Is this so? Why is it different?

Well, SHAPE's not a work of fiction, and it's something I forced myself to work at every day as a sort of diary.

You're not gripped by anything then?

Well, yes. I've got to a stage where at any time I've noted down outlines for five or six novels; I mull them over and then finally work on one. But it has to be the one I'm most gripped with, otherwise I can't do it. Writing doesn't get any easier. You'd think that the more novels you write the easier it gets but in fact it gets harder because you set yourself new problems if you're actually interested in *writing* as opposed to just selling to Ace, whoever. You spend a lot of time thinking; now what's going to interest me sufficiently to carry me through the next six months of writing? That question gets more and more difficult to answer.

What about anxiety levels? Do you still have them to any degree when you're starting a new book?

No, I don't have any anxiety. I'd probably be an anxious guy if I didn't write, but on the whole I'm fairly relaxed; when I have a story materialising I start worrying about the characters. Then I'm all right, I'm worrying about them and not me – just a sort of obsessional occupation I have.

Could you tell us more about your new fantasy cycle, 'The Day We Embarked for Cythera'*

It is a short story I'm pleased with. Sometimes when you've written something you feel that it hasn't meaning for you. Sometimes it seems to have the true elixir. And the more I thought about that story, the more I liked it, the sorrier I was that I had put in the interpolated bits of menace with the machines taking over.

Would you class it as fantasy?

Without those machine bits, it's manifestly fantasy.

You wouldn't object to a fantasy tag on it then?

No. Having written 'Cythera'. I then thought, 'Here's a perfect fantasy world awaiting exploration. Peaceful, picturesque, rather shoddy around the edges'. I have now

---

* *A short story which contained the gem of the novel,*
THE MALACIA TAPESTRY.

written four more stories around it. That was at the beginning of last year when I was rather ill with hepatitis and not feeling up to doing a novel; I couldn't concentrate. I thought I would write a series of short stories based on that little world of Cythera. Or Malacia, as it came to be called. So I sketched it out in more detail and intended to make it a sort of city-state, predominantly eighteenth century and Italian, but also with nice things like primitive steam engines and little dinosaurs and what-not in it. I only got around to writing four stories, and was going to wait and see if I could possibly write twelve. I finally sent one to Damon Knight and said (I've got another project going with Damon) they've all four got titles of Tiepolo etchings, some real, some fictitious, and the first one was called – oh shit, which was the first one . . . 'Castle Scene with Penitents,' no, 'Serpent Burning on an Altar', that's right. There's a little etching by Tiepolo, a strange thing, people digging Punchinellos out of the ground, and wicked toad-like magicians with enormous . . .(*Tape hiss drowns out description, enormous what, Brian?*) Absolutely fantastic, all executed in the 1760s . . .

Ballard uses a similar method as inspiration for some of his stories, only he uses Dali and the surrealists.

I wonder if he does? Maybe. Max Ernst and things. Yes.

It seems to me you're doing the same kind of thing, but with a different school of painters.

Yes. I wasn't thinking along those lines at first. Although there is the painting by Fragonard called THE EMBARKATION FOR CYTHERA.

Yes, we've seen this one.

With little figures lingering by the lake in one last embrace – oh, a lovely, poignant thing! That was the inspiration for the first story. Eventually they do embark and they're going back to some sort of reality. Later, the inspiration was Tiepolo's etchings, mentioned in THE SHAPE OF FURTHER THINGS. I've been trying to buy one, but they are more expensive than I thought. They had some in Agnew's . . . Eight hundred pounds! Anyhow, 'Serpent Burning on an Altar' – that was the first story, and I sent it to Damon, who was charming about it. I said: "Please don't buy it unless you really like it." I didn't tell him why, but he wrote back and said, "All right, Brian, I really like it and I'll buy it." So I said, "Right, well, there are three more waiting for you. Will you buy them too?" (*Laughs*) And he did. He's going to publish them, whether rightly or wrongly I don't know, all in one batch in a future ORBIT anthology.

In one of your letters to me you said you were a little despondent about these because you had no reaction to them. Presumably you had farmed them out to other publishers?

I sat on them for a year and then I sent them to my agent, Hilary Rubinstein. And you know, they're nothing, they don't fit into any classification. They are not overtly erotic, they are not science fiction, they are not sword and sorcery. They are too bloody long for people who might have accepted them if they were shorter. There was no one around who would publish them. And this, I thought, was quite decisive. What do you do in the end? You send them to a science fiction editor because he will take a risk when no one else will. Once they had been sent to PLAYBOY . . . Well, they aren't PLAYBOY's thing, are they?

This kind of story would have been ideal for that anthology you were in a year or two ago, THE INNER LANDSCAPE.

Yes, it would have been.

'Beware Religion!' *The one that got included was really out of place in that book.*

It was just shovelled in. It was something that Mike Moorcock wanted in a hurry. But it's quite educational to find that something that can't be categorised is so hard to sell. The Malacia stories are perfectly straightforward, nothing esoteric; they are very sweet and simple to read. No one wanted them till Damon did his stuff. I don't know where 'The Day We Embarked for Cythera' was submitted to before Mike bought it. I think I have a list. It went to a lot of places. Heaven knows, my agent may even have submitted it to ANALOG! (*Laughs*)

I find that incredible. To me they seem so commercial. While admittedly being odd, they should still strike a response in the aware reader.

I would have said so. Basically, the premise is that there are certain people whose lives are charmed and invulnerable. Shoddy things can be going on around the edges; people dying, and plague, and soldiers marching off to war; but at the centre there's always the saving grace of egotism that keeps life sweet and happy.

Which science fiction writers do you yourself admire?

Well I'm an old, hardened case. I don't like many of them, that's the honest truth.

Do you still read science fiction?

Yes, I do. I've read more this year than I've read in years – for BILLION YEAR SPREE.

Do you like David Lindsay?

No, I don't. I like William Hope Hodgson, despite all his shortcomings, his archaic speech.

And HOUSE ON THE BORDERLAND?

All those marvellous chapters where time goes by and he's transfixed at the window. That's tremendous.

What is it you don't like about Lindsay? His clumsy use of English?

All his people, Numbskull, Mashskull, and all the rest. I don't know what it's all about. I've just tried to re-read it for BILLION YEAR SPREE. What is it you like about it?

It would take too long. Colin Wilson and Visiak recommend it as a deeply religious book, even an almost mystical experience.

That is what C. S. Lewis said.

Yes, everybody who's read and understood it is pushing the religious aspect.

C. S. Lewis failed to persuade me and I doubt if anyone else will ever persuade me.

I think you have a blind spot for hard fantasy. Kingsley Amis has this too.

I think there's good reason. Science fiction always has some sort of touchstone in reality. Anything can happen in fantasy, and so one's never surprised by it. Suddenly a severed head will talk or a sword will get up of its own volition and stab someone. They're just not effects I can use in writing myself; if you're a writer you generally end by liking the sort of things you think you can do yourself. You begin sweet and innocent, reading everything, enjoying everything. Gradually you narrow down to the things that you can feed on yourself. There are writers you can draw nourishment from and writers you can't.

Well who do you draw nourishment from?

I was telling David earlier that I've just read Stapledon's STARMAKER. Fantastic. Christ . . . There's a Dover book edition with LAST AND FIRST MEN and STARMAKER in it. Those really are staggering novels indeed. The sort of ultimate classic science fiction novel. A human spirit finally meets the Starmaker and has this vision not just of our present universe, but all the ones the Starmaker started with. Incredible universes that are stored away like old toys in a toy cupboard. A glimpse is given of them. Some of the early ones were so flimsy they haven't even got dimension, they have music or something like music instead. And then the later universes! You think, 'Oh, I can't hold anymore!' But Olaf Stapledon goes on and tells you about the next universes to follow ours! Just amazing. I'm only glad I didn't read it many years ago because you can't go any further than that. STARMAKER's really the sort of ultimate novel, embracing all religion and cosmology.

It's a complete novel without any form of characterisation at all. It's very odd in that aspect.

Stapledon refuses to say it's a novel. He calls it a poetic essay or a philosophical essay or something. Thereby avoiding the issue of whether it's a novel or not. But it's much more difficult to sustain a readers interest in something like that if it has not got any characters.

That's why it's unusual. There's nothing for the reader to latch on to. There's nobody to identify with, yet it still holds.

It's so daring. You've got to be compelled by his ideas and language; there's nothing else there. Stapledon's thrown it all away and gone for the ultimate thing. A very daring book.

What are your views on religion?

I could give you my David Frost thing now, couldn't I?

In your books you don't seem to believe in a religious God as such; yet you have that 'as if it were planned' sort of mood.

Well I've got a religious sense of life, that's true. I don't believe in the regulation God. That is to say intellectually; the emotional side of you speaks as well. I've got a good friend, Robert Baldick, tremendously talented. He's at Pembroke College in Oxford. He lectures in French literature. He translated the French novels for Penguin Classics – Zola, Balzac and so on. Also Verne's TWENTY THOUSAND LEAGUES UNDER THE SEA. A marvellous chap. So nice, with a smashing second wife, an American girl. They found out that he's got a brain tumour at the beginning of this year. Such a waste! A brilliant brain there. I don't know . . . He's obviously not got very long to live. Margaret and I heard the news from his wife. And I was storming around in a terrible rage, shaking my fists upwards and saying, "You bastard! You bastard! What the hell do you think you are doing up there?" And Margaret said to me, "Come on, you know there's no one up there!"*

But when you're emotional you think on a different level from the intellectual. It seems to me proven that there can't be anyone up there! A prime-mover all right,

* *Robert Baldick died only three weeks after this conversation was taped. He was forty-four.*

109

someone who presses the button. Surely we are of a generation that accepts our earth as a sort of spaceship where everything has been recycled? Using the sun as a power source is now a very simple idea, but was highly esoteric at the turn of the century. Now we understand that all the stuff of earth, in various combinations, is used over and over again. What is it in Omar Khayyam? 'I sometimes think there never blooms so red a rose as where some buried Caesar bled'. Early example of recycling. If you accept this then there's nothing to individual life, to one generation – it's just part of an endless cycle. As the dinosaurs have been ground down, so the human species will eventually be ground down. There's nothing technology can do about that. Technology is itself a tiny part of this monstrous process, and that's that. We are all going to be ground down. That's the way it's got to be. And to think that Anyone takes particular cognisance of this, except to look down occasionally and say, "Huh, the brew's still brewing down there!" is rather laughable.

How, or were you, influenced in any way, or did you write any stories specifically for the New Wave when it developed? I ask this because your writing seemed to undergo a change around about then.

I think I did undergo a change. I suddenly thrust off what for me were rather fruitless years. I got married again. Life began anew.

There had been some doubtful novels around then, hadn't there?

I started quite well, with THE BRIGHTFOUNT DIARIES first of all, SPACE, TIME AND NATHANIEL, NON-STOP and HOTHOUSE. From then on, I was on the run for several years. Then things settled down and I could think, get on with life again. And I believe my writings improved. In fact, when I was writing BAREFOOT IN THE HEAD, the first section, 'Just Passing Through', was something I did to humour Bonfiglioli. "Oh Brain," he said, "people writ so dreadfully. Just write me a little story. Please won't you?" So I produced this short, rather horrible story. And then became obsessed with the tremendous theme of everyone on drugs. It was just when the drug thing was coming in and the idea seemed worthwhile investigating. I suppose it comes back to the religious question: how do you achieve vision in a non-God world? Maybe it should be through drugs? By the end of the novel I'd reached the decision that really drug-culture leads backwards, a backward step. Mankind shouldn't abandon any of the precious things it's gained, like intellect and art; I saw abandonment to drugs as a soft-centred thing that wouldn't get mankind anywhere. I let myself go in those stories, and was encouraged by Michael Moorcock. When I sent the second one, not to Bonfiglioli but to Mike, 'Multivalue Motorway', he got a lot of charge out of it and said, "O.K. Send me more." And I got shitty letters from people saying, "Come on, you bastard, what are you writing this rubbish for? Go back and do NON-STOP again!" An impossible demand. There you are! That was enough. I put all that I thought and felt at that time into BAREFOOT. I was writing it for about two and a half years. I know there are many scientific ideas in it. Unfortunately, of course, at first people just see the style, they don't see the content. But again I felt as I did in THE DARK LIGHT YEARS that if you're going to build a living novel then it's no good writing a diagram. You've got to be in there with the people, you've got to try and think as your characters do, hence understand the way everyone talks, submerge yourself.

What do you think of Moorcock's Jerry Cornelius, Brian?

Oh I don't really know. I think it's a good idea, and maybe THE FINAL PROGRAMME is Mike's nicest novel, but then there's a lot of Mike in that one.

THE FINAL PROGRAMME is, partly, Elric re-written.

So everyone says. I'm in the fortunate position of not reading Elric, so I don't notice that. Moorcock, despite his flamboyance, is genuinely modest. His diffidence will not always let him come through; if he ever gave a pure blast of Moorcock the heavens would probably resound. What we get is intermittent Moorcock. You know, every now and then Moorcock's revealing too much of himself, so he closes the shutters and you get a bit more TARZAN ADVENTURES or something.

He probably revealed more of himself in BEHOLD THE MAN than he had intended.

I think so. I'll tell you of something I'm doing now. I've got a project on called HELL'S CARTOGRAPHERS. I derived the idea, really, from THE SHAPE OF FURTHER THINGS. I thought that more science fiction writers ought to write about themselves and that it's perfectly legitimate to be interested in how writers write, particularly in fandom where everybody sort of has a hand in the process. I typed out a coaxing page, buttering them up as you have to do with writers, saying, 'If only Shakespeare had left a short memoir of himself how indebted we would be. And as the Shakespeares of tomorrow it's up to us science fiction writers, since no one else is damn well interested, to provide their own little memoir. I sent this note to Harry Harrison, I sent it to Damon Knight, I sent it to Fred Pohl and Bester and they all said yes. With unqualified enthusiasm they thought it was a good idea, and would write a memoir. I would have liked to have sent my proposal to Ballard, but I believed that would have been an impossible proposition. I sent it to Mike. You know, Mike's life is very interesting and if he would only just write about it it would be fascinating to read. After a long time I got a hurried postcard saying, 'Dear Brian, Genuinely grateful; terribly flattered but absolutely can't. Far too modest.' That's Moorcock. Blast it, he is modest! You know, there are writers within a stone's throw of here who would leap at the chance. But Moorcock can't bear it. So I wrote him a long letter explaining all he had to do, no self-praise, just talk about the important things that have gone on, founding the BSFA, his writing, Scandinavia, New Worlds, the things he's been involved with. But I haven't heard from him and I don't think he'll do it.

HELL'S CARTOGRAPHERS sounds interesting. Do you think it will get off the ground?

Yes. There are plenty of other people who would come in on it despite all its obvious pitfalls; not everyone can encompass autobiography. Keith Freeman said to me, "Terrible about Ted Carnell. Do you realise that you are one of the few old timers left?" I didn't know about fandom until I started writing. I still feel parvenu here! But it's true, and another generation is coming up. God, we'll all seem like dinosaurs in a few years. Let's get it down, engrave it on stone, let people read it, pick the bones out of it, see what we were about.

You were telling me earlier that you were well advanced with your latest novel. What is it called?

Yes, the first draft's written. It's a sort of space-opera. It's called THE EIGHTY MINUTE HOUR – A SPACE OPERA. You remember I told you it had a very complicated plot. People actually go to the planets – you've never had that in an Aldiss story before! Scenes set on Mars. All sorts of hopeful and horrible things are in it. For instance total contraception has been introduced, the CapCom treaty has just been signed. The CapCom treaty is an agreement between the USA and the USSR to live friendly for the next thousand years; and to cement this relationship they decide to restore the old landbridge between Europe and Asia, so they build a dam across the Bering Straits. You know a Russian buddy of mine has actually written a book about some such possibility: a grandiose engineering project with only the capitalists standing in the way. In the novel, the dam gets built; and, of course, this means the Pacific is very much warmer: there's no Alaskan current. So the Soviets can open up their Far East and the Americans can exploit Alaska. All the Pacific trading community is going very strong, Japan, South Korea, Australia way down there. Meanwhile, the Atlantic community is declining and decaying since the Arctic Ocean has been trapped. But Britain's been blown up anyway; all that's left of Britain is the Koh-I-Noor, everything's blasted to hell. A little fragment of the Tower of London survives and the Koh-I-Nor is washed up on the shores of Brittany. The USA and the USSR find that the international dateline gets in the way so they're having it moved from the Pacific over to the Atlantic, to the great discomfort of everyone thereabouts. There are various things – not only political – which I bring in, all sorts of ideas I've had around for a long time. Plus a drinking scene to end all drinking scenes. And every now and then, to justify the sub-title, people stop and sing. They all have arias.

Oh come on Brian, you're sending it up.

No. No. It's true, absolutely straight-forward science fiction. They all sing songs. One's called 'Evolution's bothering me', a very jolly thing.

Are you sending it to Ace? (Laughter)

No, I won't. It's going to be about two hundred thousand words long by the time I've finished it. I was so keen on it that I had to practically tear myself away and go to the States; I got my typist to type it out and send it to me airmail so that I could work on it in California. It came, and I didn't even unwrap it – just too much going on. That's how it stays until I finish off BILLION YEAR SPREE. But directly I finish BILLION YEAR SPREE, which will be at the end of June, 1972, it's back to THE EIGHTY MINUTE HOUR.

Are you happy with BILLION YEAR SPREE?

Oh yes. It's full of lovely stuff. It's the pure quill about the history of science fiction as I've worked it out in my little mind. Not a book primarily for the fans. That's ridiculous. It's a book for the general reader telling them what they've been missing all this time. Not saying how great it is, admitting much of it's bloody awful. But pointing out what's valuable about it, what's fun, what's interesting, stuff they should have known long ago. It's all in there, a joyous read.

You're not using it as a serious critical vehicle then?

Well, it's a serious critical vehicle. I mean I can't write it without performing an act of criticism – if by nothing else, by omission. There are certain people that I'm absolutely dead to as writers, so I don't say too much about them. It's going to be a lop-sided book, lop-sided with enthusiasm.

What do you think of SOLARIS?

I would like it a lot better if I hadn't heard such a lot of praise from second-rate critics. It is a nice strong book and that's quite a striking idea about the sentient ocean. I don't believe that the English translation does it justice. Somewhere in the middle of the book there's a serious gulf I can't quite think what it is . . . a lack of human tone . . . I like another Polish writer better, a chap called Slavomir Mrożek.

Brian, how do you feel about the lack of an outlet for

*writers. We don't have a regular magazine for science
fiction in Britain. Does this disturb you?*

It doesn't disturb me personally.

*No, but we do have a situation at the moment where
established authors find it relatively easy to get their work
published but we don't seem to have a breeding ground
for new talent.*

From that point of view it's extremely bad. I can't see at
the moment what sort of magazine is wanted and if one
could see, then there might be a viable possibility of
producing it. Not a VISIONS OF TOMORROW type
magazine. I would like to see more general magazines
which published SF among other stories; but the day of
such magazines is largely past. Paperbacks have gradually
superseded them.

*Ken Bulmer had the right idea with SWORD AND
SORCERY, though not necessarily with that title.*

Maybe so. That's for you, not me.

*Do you feel that it would have been a commercial success,
that it would have sold?*

I'm sure it would. Ken Bulmer would have been a damn
good editor. Though what worries me now – things are
being done about this – is what happens to Ted Carnell's
series NEW WRITINGS IN SF. (*This series is now being
edited by Ken Bulmer.*)

I've never really been happy with this series.

It's pretty awful. But there's a chance yet. Sweet old Ted,
he really didn't know one end of a story from the other.
If someone else took it over, and I know who Corgi has in
mind, then that would be something people in the field
would like a lot more. It's selling like mad at the moment,

dull though it is. Corgi are happy with it, they don't want to let it die. Now they've got up to twenty, they're reprinting the early ones *and* they are doing the Best of the Best . . . You know.

They are appalling collections, that's true, but the paperback format seems to be the only viable way of selling magazines. But it's still an opportunity for new writers to display their talent.

What makes it an opportunity particularly for new writers is that the books have to appear regularly; they've got to be filled with whatever happens to be available. Damon Knight has an irregular schedule, or pretty irregular, with ORBIT – he can wait until he's got the material he wants; and so that's cheating! But Carnell's NEW WRITINGS IN SF had to be published twice a year – he was always mildly desperate. Obviously Ted often got a lot of bum stories. I found the same when I first began selling to him for NEW WORLDS. I remember sending him a story which I thought well of, called 'The Failed Men'. I got a letter back by return saying, "Dear Brian, this will amuse you. I was going to reject your story, which I think is awful, but I found I'd got a gap of five thousand words, so it's going to be in the next issue." Oh yes, I was so amused by a letter like that . . .(*Laughs*) Terrible. Oh God, Carnell was so depressing.

Everyone holds him in such respect though. They still say he was a good anthologist.

He was here, and no one else was doing anything, so such talent as there was gravitated towards him. But there were special things about Ted. For one thing his extraordinary niceness.

I wasn't really talking about him as a person, but as an editor.

Ah, but it rubs off, don't you see? One disruptive shit at the top can really foul up our little world of science fiction – that's absolutely true. But Ted was an exceptionally nice guy and ordinarily honest. He would never swindle you out of a halfpenny. Very honest, very gentlemanly to deal with. Never swore, just had a gin and tonic on a Sunday. Highly respectable. The publishers and the other agents liked him immensely. I wrote his obituary in THE TIMES saying as much, because it was very important. Most people, when they thought of science fiction in the publishing world, thought, 'I'll ring up Ted Carnell'. And there wasn't someone at the other end who said, "No, I'm not going to deal with you," or who was a swindler using his writers to his own crooked ends . . . Ted had a sense of tact, and quite honestly, if he'd been an awful cheapskate like, oh I don't know, whoever was a cheap-skate – name your favourites – the picture would be very different. But without literary skill he built his business up gradually. Any writer over thirty at this convention went through Ted at one time or another, and they always had the same good experience. Eventually you had to get away from Ted because he was too nice to deal with publishers. He'd never screw them and say, "Come on, this guy is starving. Pay him two hundred and fifty pounds instead of a hundred." So the writers were starving. But everyone left him in the nicest possible manner, after awful heart-searching. Mike did it, Ballard did it. Even Ballard who can be so ferocious was gentle breaking away from Ted. Everyone did it with a terrific amount of finesse. With one exception whom we won't name who just about had a lawsuit. Ted kept everything very sweet behind the scenes; this is why, on the whole, whatever the difference between British writers, they may hate each other's point of view, or hate each other personally, but they all agree to behave civily in public. Carnell didn't turn up much at conventions, but there was always Carnell around. You did actually love the man. A very different kettle of fish from Campbell – Carnell never originated an idea. No, that's not entirely true, sometimes he did. I suppose he encouraged James White to go and to write those endless Sector General stories. That must have been a Carnell idea. He certainly encouraged me to write NON-STOP as a novel. On the whole he was a very quiet man who didn't give out much; but he kept everything going. He was a good positive force.

What do you think of Moorcock as an editor?

Moorcock had the genuine flame. When that thing happened Moorcock really did his nut. Very nice, very rare thing to see. Maybe now the flame has gone out. I don't find the quarterlies exciting. NEW WORLDS was genuinely exciting, however much nonsense was in it along with the nourishment.

Do you think that it was the pressure placed upon him that made the flame go out or was it just a drifting away?

It may have been that as well. The love affair was too hot not to cool down!

I think it was the only way he could keep the quarterly alive by having no really unconventional stuff in it.

In a way. He's not here now because he's writing six novels, writing off the debt to the printer that he incurred over the old NEW WORLDS. You know the history of ARKHAM HOUSE. In a bibliography of ARKHAM HOUSE August Derleth relates the story of his struggles. And he says 'Contrary to the generally accepted opinion that I was living off the writings of H. P. Lovecraft, I funnelled in . . .' Oh some enormous sum of money, through his own hack writing, to keep the publishing company going. Tremendous dedication that. Twenty-five thousand dollars over ten years, or something like that.

ARKHAM HOUSE would print say two thousand copies of books like THE DARK MAN or NIGHT'S BLACK AGENTS, and it might take six or seven years to get rid of them. Ridiculous.

Yes, that's sad. None of it went to Derleth of course. That's a bad thing. Also he inspired all the other houses. SHASTA and GNOME and the rest started up after ARKHAM HOUSE. People took courage from Derleth's example. And again to come back to Ted, people took courage from Ted, because however dull those magazines were they had one prime virtue, they appeared regularly. No one else managed to do that. You could go to the bookstalls and there they were on time, the same shaggy old writers in there. All those frantic people, E. R. James and Francis G. Reyer.

It's amazing, you flick through some of those old magazines from the fifties and you can't help but wonder where are they all now?

They've gone back into the woodwork. Ready to live again, just bring back VISIONS OF TOMORROW and they'll all come scuttling out. You know, Beep! Beep! Beep! Their little antennae going, smelling some horrible cheap market. (*Pause*) There's a tremendous sense of continuity in science fiction. Christ, I've said as much against fandom as anyone, but it's that central core of enthusiasm which keeps things going. Guys who come in as fans, who eventually rise up to become editors – look at Fred Pohl there, distinguished fellow, he was running about in knickerbockers editing a magazine at thirteen, or something equally preposterous. He was just another fan. And presumably that's the way it will continue. There's something awful, something subversive, about science fiction which most readers can't bear. It needs people with enthusiasm just to keep it going.

This interview took place at the 1972 Easter SF Convention.

HARLAN ELLISON

Eggsucker

A Prequel to 'A Boy and His Dog'

---

*World War III lasted from 25 June 1950 when the
Republic of Korea was invaded by 60,000 screaming
North Korean troops spearheaded by something in excess
of 100 Russian-built tanks . . . to 1 January 1983 when
the Vatican* Entente Cordiale *was signed between the
Eastern and Western blocs. World War III – hot and cold
– lasted thirty-three years. Then it was over.*

*World War IV lasted five days, until the few remaining
missiles that had jammed in their release phase had left
their silos beneath the Painted Desert and the Urals and
the Gobi Altay; and by then there wasn't much of anything left to fight over. Five days.*

*Then, what was left belonged to anybody who wanted
it, anybody who had a taste for radiation and rubble. But
it was a very different world. The 'good folks' sank their
caisson cities, their sterile downunders deep in the earth.
And the snaggle-toothed remnants of the cities were
abandoned to the survivors, vicious roverpaks of parent-
less young boys . . . and their telepathic dogs.*

– As Blood tells it.

Unless I've dropped a stitch at some point and have
messed up the chronology, I met Vic – whom I permit to

---

wallow in the delusion that he is my 'master' – in 2021. The year of what they once knew as their Lord, 2021. As solos go, Vic is okay. He'll never be Bertrand Russell in the celebration department, their Lord knows, but he's steadfast, responsible and game as they come. A bit *too* game, occasionally. The kid takes too many chances to suit my highly-attuned sense of survival.

The way Vic tells it, he found me.

Having long-since learned the twists and turns of the labyrinth that is the human ego, I permit him to batten on this monstrous inaccuracy.

A little self-delusion goes a long way to keeping one's pet human in line.

It also permits them a rat hole of dignity-preservation into which they can scurry, when they're put in their place. To be specific, I remember an evening.

We had found a case of bottles in what was left of a Mayfair Market. Half a dozen were still intact with the contents unevaporated. (When I discovered what the contents were composed of, I realised the liquid was probably non-biodegradable unto the hundredth generation.) Six bottles of a virulent jet fuel substitute labelled Sweet Betsy Pike fruit wine, 92° proof, distilled from grain, rare earths and unnameable trace metals, helium, argon, rutabaga and Necco wafers. I would sooner have swilled my own piss.

But good old Albert, aka Vic, whooped and howled like a Belgian wolfhound getting a glucose enema. "This booze is worth its weight in ammo!" he yowled, capering around the dirt-banked pit, all that remained of the basement of the Mayfair Market. As he danced, he did a little sidestep so he wouldn't trip over the bodies of the two rovers he'd had to waste to gain possession of the Sweet Betsy Pike fruit wine. One of them wasn't quite dead, kept jerking his right leg the way I do when I'm sleeping and having a bad dream. The other one was spread out a bit; really a messy shot; way below Vic's standard between-the-eyes.

So we took the six bottles in a wrap-up and went looking for Skipper and Walter, who were the ramrods of a roverpak called The 82nd Airborne. They called them-selves that for who knows what reason, maybe they'd seen that old movie, I think it was a Van Johnson flick, maybe it was *Geronimo* or *Gung Ho*, or something like that. Vic is the movie buff, not me. Mostly I'm bored by flicks, un-less they're about food.

The 82nd Airborne was the armourer for most of the roverpaks, except for Fellini and that bunch of teenaged pederastees he uses for slaves. Freaky as Fellini is, he's smart; and he'd found his own secret cache of ammuni-tion, which was one of the things that made him the single strongest roverpak in the area. They're kidnappers and mean shitty killers – they do it for chuckles, not because they have to – so nobody crosses him. He's also dead chill on solos who might get to some excavatable food before his gang does, so nobody goes near him. So except for that creep Fellini, The 82nd Airborne kept everyone in slugs. That was their barter. But you had to bring Skipper and Walter something valuable – not to mention your empty brass which they used for making reloads – before they'd fill you up again.

Vic seemed to think that a few bottles of diabetically sweet poison was heavy bartering coin. He was right, of course. He has a good sense about that kind of thing. Not me. I can never figure out what makes humans go for one kind of awful tasting slop over some other equally noxious crap. I once brought Vic a dead sparrow and suggested he use it to get us fresh water. He looked at me as if I was crazy. "People don't eat dead birds, Blood," he said. He was trying to be patient.

"And why is that, Albert," I said, being cranky.

"Stop calling me Albert!" I love to hear Vic scream. And since he's never quite understood why I get such a kick out of calling him Albert – after Albert Payson Terhune, who wrote all those stupid dog books in which we noble creatures were pets, always being saved by some sappy human – it is my best gambit to make him scream.

"Okay, so *why*, master Vic?"

"Because dead bird is *lousy* tasting, that's why."

"But you eat sheep, and cow, and snake. I've even seen some of you eat French fried rat."

"Yeah?" he said, nastily. "Well, there are even low scumbags who think parboiled *dog* is a delicacy. Keep fucking with me and I'll trade *you* for fresh water."

And he walked away, leaving the dead sparrow on the sidewalk. So did I. Yecchhh.

Anyhow, we took the Sweet Betsy Pike fruit wine over near what used to be the docks, and Vic yelled out across the harbour, "Hey! Skipper! Walter!"

And after a while a light went on, over there on the big barge in the middle of the harbour, this barge that used to be a garbage scow, but which Skipper and Walter and The 82nd Airborne had taken over for their home turf, where they had all the lathes and the reloading presses and the die sets for reloading brass set up. And somebody, maybe Skipper, but I couldn't tell across the water, used a megaphone and yelled back, "Yeah, who is it? Whaddaya want?"

And Vic yelled back that it was him and Blood, and he had barter, and the voice asked across the water what kind of ammo Vic needed, and Vic said .22 longs and .45s, and the voice asked what he had to trade, and Vic yelled back that he had booze, and the megaphone voice took a beat as if he was asking someone else if it was cool, and then hollered over that they'd send the skiff. So we waited in the dark, sitting on the edge of the jetty, looking out across the harbour, all that inky water, and I passed the time by trying to run Vic through his lessons.

"Name the Presidents of the United States after Franklin D. Roosevelt," I said.

Vic kicked at the water. He didn't answer.

"After Roosevelt," I insisted.

"Don't want to," he said, fishing around in his left-to-right bandolier for a cigarette butt.

"What's the matter, brain in repose at this time?"

131

"Get off me." There was a miserable tone in his voice.

"Come on, take a crack at it. I'll get you started: Truman, Eisenhower . . ."

He filched up a butt from one of the bandolier pockets, along with his flint and steel, and sparked himself alight. *"Truman, Eisenhower . . ."* I said again, a little tougher.

He turned on me sharply and looked down where I was sitting in the dark. "God damn you, Blood! Truman, Eisenhower, Kennedy, Johnson, Nixon, Carter, Brown, Kennedy, Kennedy, Kennedy, I told you I didn't want to do it!"

He was yelling.

"You forgot Ford," I said. Quietly.

"Oh, piss off!" And he got up and walked away.

I didn't know what was lumbering him. We hadn't had a bad day; it had been a pretty good one, in fact. A couple of cans of salt beef and some canned cherries from that Mayfair Market, we had a pretty secure flop for the night, a janitor's apartment tucked back at the rear of an alley under a blasted apartment building, with only one channel of attack in case someone came after us. Not a bad day.

I got up and followed him.

"Hey," I said, finding him easily in the dark. "What's on your mind, kiddo?"

He pulled on the cigarette butt till it was so short I wondered if it was singeing the little hairs in his nose. I plopped my tail down and waited. After a second he snapped the butt off his thumb and forefinger, it went spiralling off into the ink and made a *pssss* in the harbour. When he spoke, I knew he was thinking about other places, other times. "Hell, I don't know, Blood. Just feeling very crummy. One of those rovers this afternoon, the one kept saying please please please when I shot him. No women for almost a month. All this history and crap you keep whipping on me till my head hurts. Every day's just like every other day, just hustling for food."

My pet boy was suffering from battle fatigue.

"Come on down here so we can talk face to face." He

132

crouched down, started scratching the fur behind my right ear automatically. I had him trained to a fine edge.

"Look, Vic: this is only temporary. One day very soon, as I keep telling you, something's going to start happening in this country. Someone's going to settle down and start a farm, start planting things right in the ground, put up a stout guard wall around the homestead to keep out creeps like Fellini, and then after a while someone else will join him, and then there'll be two, and then a third, and after a while it'll be a real settlement. They may have started doing it already . . . the War's been over for forty years already. Unless I've dropped a stitch somewhere. But I *think* I'm sure it's forty years, give or take a couple. So maybe they've already started."

Vic snorted a half-chuckle, as if it was all bullshit.

"Come on now, kiddo," I said, keeping at it, "you've heard enough rumours from solos who've passed through, and that minstrel last year . . ."

"It's all ramadoola."

"Maybe not."

"Rumours. Bullshit. About 'over the hill' – right?"

"Perhaps. That's as good a name for Valhalla as any."

"Where's that?"

"No place. It's just a word out of mythology."

"And what's *that*?!" he snarled, getting angry at my using a word he didn't know. "Is that some more useless bullshit you're gonna try and teach me?"

"No. You have no need for mythology, old friend." It made me sad. "You'll make your own."

We sat quietly for a few minutes, waiting for the skiff. "But there's *got to be* an 'over the hill', kiddo. Take my word for it."

"Trust me . . . right?"

"That's right. Trust me."

He looked off across the harbour, where the light on the skiff had detached itself from the dark bulk of the barge, and he murmured, "Yeah, well, we ain't never gonna see it, dog." I didn't correct his grammar. He was just feeling down, feeling low; he'd get over it. A decent firefight, some sex, he'd be okay again. I didn't even object when he called me dog. But I'd get him later: call him 'boy'.

Then I'd tell him about Tarzan.

And after that I'd teach him about mythology.

The skiff slid in at the jetty and there were three skinny rovers levelling pump guns at us. We walked back and they braced us. "Spread," said the one in the prow. Vic didn't lie down and spread. He stood there with the .22 in the crook of his arm, the flap of the .45's holster unbuttoned. He just stared back at them. The one in the middle had a lantern. It didn't give much light, but they could see he wasn't about to let them frisk him. "Spread," the skinny pump gun in the prow said again.

"You're here, so that means Skipper and Walter sent you over, and that means they know me, and they know I'm okay, so stop playing Clint Eastwood and move your ass so we can get in."

They faced each other that way for a couple of long moments and I thought, oh shit, they always have to do their *machismo* number. And I calculated how far and how high I'd have to jump to get at the throat of the skinny in the middle with the lantern. But the pump gun in the prow nodded, and backed off, so we got in the skiff.

And they took us over the water to the barge.

Everybody forgot Ford.

I'm still telling about this evening I remember.

We got over to the barge, and it was the first time I ever saw the tiniest sign that humans could be friendly to one another. Vic actually *shook hands* with Skipper and Walter.

Skipper was a short kid, perhaps seventeen, with straight brown hair that he greased back flat to his head. He had a nice pair of blue eyes that watched everything. His hands were small but they were fast. I could see where he would have decided to play it safe, running a roverpak, rather than going solo. He had the kind of hands I've come to recognise on humans who like to make things.

Walter was funny. He was pudgy and didn't say anything that made sense. He whistled a lot and sometimes sang bits and snatches of old songs. Every once in a while he'd come over and hug or kiss Skipper. They were friends, and it rubbed off on the rest of The 82nd Airborne. And Vic.

They took the four bottles of wine Vic offered and all the brass Vic had policed up, and the deal was made. Then Skipper suggested Vic hang out and get ripped with some of them, and Vic said he'd put up the other two bottles, and they proceeded to get themselves cross-eyed, so quickly, that it only reaffirmed my opinion of people. I was sorry to see Vic in that state, however. He is a very sloppy drunk.

Which was when he made his mistake with me, which was when I had to put him in his place, which was where I began with this anecdote.

One of Skipper and Walter's workmen came out of the factory area at the rear of the barge and gave Vic a boot full of loads, and Vic dumped them into his sack, and kissed Walter, and so to me, "Hey, Blood, have a drink."

I just looked at him. He had said it aloud, not with his mind, silent, the way we talk most of the time. He'd said it aloud so all the rest of them could hear it. I just looked at him. There are times when Vic is in really tacky taste.

"Whassa matter?" Skipper said. "He don't wanna drink with us? Too good to drink with us? Dogs ain't s'posed to drink with us? Somethin' wrong he don't wanna drink with us?"

He wasn't a surly lush, he was just rambling. But Vic knew better. I don't drink. I don't use dope. I have sworn a vow of sexual abstinence. One of us has to be pure, so we can *hope* to stay alive. Also, I am a noble creature.

I thought at Vic, "That was a stupid move."

He thought back, "Oh, take it easy, fer crissakes. Have a bite of this stuff. Good for you."

Between solos and their dogs, as between selected members of roverpaks and their dogs, the mind-to-mind is a closed channel. No one can eavesdrop. It's partially gene-tic, partially empathic, partially chemically-induced. At least it was that way during the War, when my ancestors were first altered for skirmisher duty. I suppose the solos and rovers who can 'path are the children of those troopers who were trained and innoculated to work with the skirmishers. All I know for certain is that there have only been one or two other humans with whom I've had mind-to-mind communication.

So no one else was listening to our bickering.

"I'm going for a walk," I 'pathed. "When I get back, I'd like to see you on your feet, if that's possible. I'd like to see us get off this barge and back to our flop for the night. I'd like to see you assuming a little of the respon-sibility for this partnership."

"You just hate to see me happy."

"I just hate to see you stinko."

"I'm not stinko."

"Well, you're sure as hell not pro-survival at the moment, Albert, dear chum."

Walter said, "Havin' a fight with your mutt?"

Vic looked at him. "He ain't a mutt."

"*Isn't* a mutt," I 'pathed.

"Isn't a mutt," Vic said.

"I wouldn't take no shit from no eggsucker," one of Skipper's men said. It was the pump gun from the skiff.

I got up and walked out of the room.

I don't have to take that kind of crap.

And if my alleged master can't protect my honour, well, perhaps a talented sniffer ought to find a new relationship. That's what I was thinking as I wandered into the factory section of the barge.

I was just killing time. I wandered around, looking at the Lyman reloading press and the primer seater and the powder scale and the Saeco sizing die they used for mak-ing new slugs. There were a couple of rovers working in there. One of them was bent over a C-H Tool & Die Corp. bullet swaging die set and another one was using a canneluring tool that knurls a groove around the slug for crimpling. They looked up as I came in and sat down. I like watching people work at their craft. One of the things I miss most these days is seeing a good carpenter or boot-maker practising his art.

"G'wan, get the hell out of here, you eggsucker!" one of them snarled. He threw a fistful of shavings at me; and missed. But I got up and ambled away. Metal shavings in the paw pad can be a nuisance.

That was the second time in ten minutes I'd been called an eggsucker. My mood was definitely not benevolent. The next dipshit who insulted me was, I swore, destined to go to his grave with my fangs in his throat.

I wandered around for a while, then back into the ex-quisite, sumptuous, palatial saloon of the elegant garbage scow. For rovers who lived like pigs, they sure had a high-assed opinion of themselves. Give slobs a lathe and some turning equipment and they think they're the chosen people.

Vic was still lying on his back.

Walter was asking, "What's it like out there?"

Vic looked up at him blearily. "Whaddaya mean: what's it like out there? Out where?"

"Being solo."

"Oh." He hiccuped. "Okay, I suppose."

"Bullshit," I said, mind-to-mind. Vic shrugged.

"Things're getting tighter. Most of the fast easy food you can dig up is gone. Found a Mayfair Market today . . . where I got the wine . . . had to fight to get it. Fellini's organising fast. He's got that big slave wagon of his. About two dozen good shots hanging around all the time. Won't be long."

"Waht won't be long?" Skipper asked.

"Till he takes over the city."

They seemed startled. I realised they had very little sense of history, of the passage or progression of events. What was now, was now; and anything beyond that required imagination, of which their pointy little heads had never known a taste.

Vic was different. I'd taught Vic.

"Stands to reason," Vic said, playing the big man, the teacher, slurring his words over the wine. Idiot savant. "He can't let any solos run loose because they might find the ammo and food he needs to keep feeding his people. And it's those troops of his that keep solos from putting a slug in his fat head. He loses them, if he can't feed 'em, and he's not in charge any more . . . he's just another fat old man."

"Yeah, but what's that got to do with us?" Skipper asked. "We're not solos. We're organised. We've got our own thing here, our own turf. Everybody needs us to re-load their brass."

Vic laughed. "Dream on, Skipper. Fellini doesn't need you. At least he doesn't think he does, which is the same thing."

Walter said, "Yeah, but the *other* roverpaks need us."

"For how long, man? As soon as Fellini cleans out or scares off the solos in the area, then he'll start taking over the roverpaks, one by one. He has to. Only way he can control the situation."

Skipper looked interested. "How do you know all this? Somebody lay it all on you . . .?"

"Hell, no," Vic said. "Blood told me a lot of it, and I just figured out the rest. As George Santayana said in *The Life of Reason*, 'Those who cannot remember the past are condemned to repeat it'. I've studied history. I *know* that's what will happen."

They were staring at him as if he was crazy. I'd warned Vic never to flaunt his education. It made people nervous.

The pump gun skinny said, "Where the hell'd you get all that shit?"

Vic suddenly realised, through his drunken haze, that he'd made himself look different, set himself apart. "Uh . . ."

They were all staring at us now. Skipper looked very twitchy. Vic licked his lips nervously.

"Uh . . . I got it all from Blood," he said, the miserable sonofabitch fink. Direct lineal descendant of Senator Joseph McCarthy.

The pump gun skinny bared yellow teeth, snickered, and said, "I wouldn't take all that stupid shit from no egg-sucker."

That was number three.

That was it!

Take *that*, you asshole! And I went for the mammy-jammer.

Oh, I was lovely. A furry blur of light, a death-dealing instrument of destruction, a lone noble beast defending his honour against the Philistines, a juggernaut of power and pain, up and arching out in a smooth leap that took me over Skipper's head, right past the loudmouth and into the wall of the barge. I fell down and lay there twitching. How fleeting is grandeur.

Pump gun skinny raised his weapon and threw down on me. Through blurred eyes I saw the creep curling around the trigger to blow me away. And then his head exploded and spattered all over me.

I heard Vic say, "Freeze, piss-ants!"

Then he was shuffling among them, pointing that big .45 at Skipper's skull, and he knelt down smoothly, and he was kind of manhandling me up into his free arm, and I crawled around over his shoulder and got into the ruck-sack . . . upsidedown. Then I guess I fainted.

Next thing I knew, we were on the dock and I was being jangled around like crazy, because Vic was running for our lives in the dark. I *assumed* all this, because I was wedged down with the tin cans and the rest of the crap in Vic's rucksack. But he'd gotten us out of there . . . alive . . . I was at least sure of that much.

After a while, he slowed down, and I could hear him panting like crazy. And cursing at me.

"Stupid, goddam, short-tempered, imbecilic, moron

dog! Damned near got us killed. Spoilt my night! Lost us the only armourer in the territory, goddam stupid lousy ignorant fucking *eggsucker*!"

That was number four, but I was upside-down. And half conscious. But I felt bad.

Finally, he stopped, shucked out of the knapsack, turned it over and dumped me out. We were in an alley.

It was dark. But I could feel the heat coming off him. Oh, boy, was he pissed off at *me*.

I staggered around for a minute, trying to get my left front leg to work in unison with my right rear, and finally I circled around him and sat down on some rubble. He was sitting there with his head in his hands, looking miserable.

"I was getting tired of this town, anyway," I said, hoping to cheer him up a little. It was obvious: we'd have to get out now. Nowhere to get fresh ammo, marked lousy by The 82nd Airborne, which would make us *persona non grata* with the other roverpaks who might otherwise tolerate a reliable solo and his dog.

Vic peered up at me from between his hands. It was dark but I could read him even in the dark. He didn't say anything. He just stared at me. I didn't feel too terrific.

"I hear there's some activity out around Duluth,' I said.

That was a lie. I'd heard the taconite creatures that came up out of Lake Superior would eat your ass off.

He didn't say anything. And he had his mind blocked off; but the seepage was awful. Like blood oozing out under a door jamb.

"We could try for 'over the hill' in the direction of Vermont," I said. I didn't even know if Vermont was *there* anymore.

Then we sat and stared at each other for a while.

Finally, I just decided it was better to blow off steam than to squat on my tail feeling guilty.

"Look, kiddo, it wasn't *all* my fault! If you hadn't gotten bagged, or if you hadn't let them insult me without saying anything, I wouldn't have run amuck! It's *your* responsibility, too."

"That's it," he said, quietly, and he got up. His being quiet scared the hell out of me.

Then he just walked out of the alley, right out into the middle of the street, and kept going. No cover, no checking out the turf, nothing. He just walked away from me.

I sat there for a second, and then padded to the mouth of the alley and watched him go. Just like that. We'd been together close on two years, and here was this ingrate fourteen-year-old clown thinking he could just up and walk away like that. Without even a by-your-leave or a thank you for all I'd done for him. The silly sonofabitch!

Well, let him go, I thought. Let the moron get himself chewed up by Fellini or some backshooting solo. Let *him* try sniffing out females, see how good *he* was at it. Might not matter so much at age fourteen, but wait till he hit fifteen, sixteen . . . *ha*! Seventeen! At seventeen, like every other weird human boy, he'd start running around on all fours looking for sex. And some female solo with as much muscle as him would stick a bayonet in his chest just when he was about to get on her. Serve him right, too, the asshole.

Let him go! An educated nose like mine came high these days. There were solos just *crying* for a good dog. And I worked cheap. It didn't take that much to feed me; not as much as an Akita or a Doberman. There were even roverpaks that needed a good lead dog. Even if I started at the bottom of the pile, with my talent I'd be lead dog in no time.

It wouldn't be easy. A new dog always had to eat some shit for a while before his excellence was recognised. But I could do it. Maybe a year. Maybe two. In a roverpak. Eating shit.

I decided to follow him, to tell him he was on his own. To tell him I could make it just very well thank you without a stupid boy like him running the show.

I trotted out of the alley and kept to the shadows. Even

if he was going to be stupid about survival, I still had my wits about me. The trouble on the barge hadn't been *all* my fault. He'd let them call me an eggsucker. He knew I didn't like that. And besides, the clown with the pump gun had given him trouble earlier. I knew he'd blown him away halfway because of that, not just on my account.

I was maybe a block behind him, and there he was, just staggering half-drunk down the centre of the avenue. What a schmuck!

Then I saw the glowing green haze that meant there was a screamer in a crater in the middle of the road. Vic was too juiced to even see it. But then, humans can't see the greenish-blue radiation haze as well as we noble creatures can. Go ahead, you dip, I thought, just walk on down the street and in another ten steps you're going to be hugging a screamer. Go on, walk away from me; you're not five minutes without me and already about to get burned. You toad.

Bumble, bumble, bumble, he just went careening toward the crater, and the green haze got brighter, which meant the screamer was aware my valiant ex-master was on the way. So long, turkey, I thought. That's it for you, screwloose!

And then I thought of eating shit at the bottom of a roverpak for a year or two, and the next thing I knew was running full out toward him, howling my brave little heart out. "Albert, you nincompoop! Look out! Screamer crater right in front of you! Look out, dummy! Jump it, dodge it, get away from there, you simple shit!"

But he was too drunk to know what he was doing. And there, right on schedule, coming up like something out of an old Japanese horror flick . . . there was the king awful ugliest screamer I've ever seen, oozing green slime and his parts falling off like some medieval drawing of a rotting flagellant or a leper, nothing but bitten fingernails all the way back to the knuckles, and eyelashes as long as spider legs, and big whirling eyes without eyelids, his mouth open and yelling with the pain of his burns, groping and clutching and trying to climb out of the pit . . .

And stupid Vic just sashaying up to him as if he were a chorus girl looking for a good time.

"*Look out, you asshole!*" I screamed mind-to-mind, and sailed past him on the rise, just looming up in that screamer's face and baring my fangs and barking like crazy . . .

And the poor devil fell back into the pit and I didn't have to touch him, which would have been the end of me, and I fell into the pit and didn't even stop to look around, just came up running and scrabbled like a mole up the other side and off down the street trying to beat today into tomorrow.

And here came my valiant master, the well-known brain damage case, Vic aka Albert, running along behind me, his mouth open and screaming in terror just the way that poor devil screamer had screamed, which is rotten syntax, but I was *terrified*!

The next time I stopped for breath, I was two miles up the road and way back there somewhere good old Vic was running so hard his knees were hitting him in the chin. I stopped and fell down and lay on my side in the gutter and just breathed in and out as best I could, and prayed for a better life.

Vic came running up, went fifty yards past me, realised the heap in the gutter had been me, and came back. He fell down on the kerb and panted for ten minutes.

When the lights stopped flashing and my chest stopped hurting and I stopped sounding like an asthmatic. I flipped over, got my legs under me, and sat down properly.

He was staring at me.

"You hungry?" he asked.

"I could eat."

"There's some of those canned cherries left."

"That would be all right."

He pulled a can of cherries out of the rucksack, and the can opener. "Green, wasn't he?" I said, offhandedly.

"Oh, he was okay."

"You looked as if you didn't know whether to shit or wind your watch."

"Eggsucker," he said. He was grinning.

So we just sat there and ate the canned cherries.

"Name the Presidents after Roosevelt," I said. "Franklin, not Teddy."

And he did. But he forgot Ford again. There's only so much you can do with a human. But it's a living.